Fault
Lines

Emily Itami

PHOENIX

First published in Great Britain in 2021 by Phoenix Books
This paperback edition first published in Great Britain
in 2022 by Phoenix Books,
an imprint of The Orion Publishing Group Ltd
Carmelite House, 50 Victoria Embankment
London EC4Y 0DZ

An Hachette UK Company

1 3 5 7 9 10 8 6 4 2

Copyright © Emily Itami 2021

A CIP catalogue record for this book is
available from the British Library.

ISBN (Mass Market Paperback) 978 1 4746 2026 0
ISBN (eBook) 978 1 4746 2027 7
ISBN (Audio) 978 1 4746 2028 4

Typeset by Input Data Services Ltd, Somerset

Printed in Great Britain by Clays Ltd, Elcograf S.p.A.

MIX
Paper from
responsible sources
FSC® C104740

www.orionbooks.co.uk
www.phoenix-books.co.uk

'This d   .eart . . .
Short, emot nal and very funny, Emily Itami's debut is an
unmissab   mantics everywhere'

                                    F   sc B   Stylist

'Itami captures the magic of Tokyo and makes it part of the
couple's relationship, complete with cherry blossoms, tiny
bars and excellent food . . . It punches above its weight in
its themes and the maturity with which it examines them,
such as how love intertwines with or comes up against
duty, and the feeling of having lost a part of oneself.
Although she situates these ideas in a very specific social
context, Itami manages to make them universal'   The *i*

'Exploring motherhood and Japanese culture, I found this
a fascinating and insightful read'   Nina Pottell, *Prima*

'A lyrical story about love and a fascinating look at the
collision of old and new traditions in modern Tokyo'
                                        Sarra Manning, *Red*

'What is the cost of a mother's love? In her debut novel
Fault Lines, Emily Itami explores this question with wit
and poignancy , . . dreamy . . . Itami's descriptions of
spring in Japan are to be savoured'   *New York Times*

'Provocative, spirited . . . What's intriguing about *Fault
Lines* is its shrewd commentary on Japan's societal expectations of women'   *Washington Post*

EMILY ITAMI grew up in Tokyo before moving to London, where she now lives with her young family. She has been published widely as a freelance journalist and travel writer. This is her first novel.

For T, S and J, like everything.

I

The whole Kiyoshi situation started a long time before he was ever in the picture. The way a calligraphy painting begins before the first black stroke makes it onto the page. Begins when the painter collects together scroll and brushes and grinds up the pigment, or even before that, when he (or she – and yet, in this country, it's almost invariably he) has an idea in his head of what to paint. So, the scene was already set, the pigment crushed, the painterly hand poised.

All of which suggests that it was inevitable, that Kiyoshi himself was almost irrelevant, that he could have been anyone. That I, like a pre-fluffed adult performer, was waiting indiscriminately for whoever came along. There's a part of me that believes it could only have been Kiyoshi – that if it hadn't been him, everything in my life would have continued as it was and any diversion from the path would have been effortlessly resisted. And then there are the times when I'm trying to forget about the whole sorry mess, laughing at myself so it hurts a little less, when I believe it was my own weakness that stacked the whole house of cards to start with, and it had nothing to do with

Kiyoshi at all. Wasn't Romeo madly in love with Rosaline four days before he killed himself for Juliet? What's in a name? The boy was a raging bag of hormones set to obsess over whichever nubile young creature came into his line of sight. Does anyone need to get hung up on which one it was? (But it's the ultimate love story! It's destiny, and fate, and love greater than life!) What is love anyway? What is love whatislove

whatislovewhatis loveha ha

ha

ha

ha.

Aki has a mode he goes into, where you can practically watch the hormones go into overdrive for a minute or two, where he lolls his tongue out and shakes his head from side to side and runs around the room as if he's got fleas. Behaving exactly like a dog on heat. I've seen his daddy do the same thing, which is difficult to imagine when you see him reigning, magnificent and still, from the splendour of his enormous desk in his enormous office. Maybe it's contagious, something you catch from your husband and your son, because recently I've been feeling that a lot, the urge to run around like a dog chasing its tail, asking myself stupid questions and trying to shake them out of my head.

Trying to shake them out of my head because, as an advert on the Tokyo Metro reminded me the other day, *Life's What You Make It!* It was advertising a washing powder that can make you float in a white shift dress across a blue sky. Or possibly it was an advert for anti-constipation medicine or life insurance. It's hard to tell. I'm always at my most open-minded, not to say

2

emotionally susceptible, on the Metro – it's the lurking possibility of death by earthquake that does it. It doesn't make me feel any calmer that the Namboku line is the deepest in Tokyo; I have no idea whether this makes it more or less likely that in the event of an earthquake all the walls would cave in, and have never been able to get a clear answer about it out of anyone. I realise that to be a die-hard inhabitant of this city, you're expected to smile demurely in the face of the almighty fault line that runs straight through it and place complete trust in whatever dinky gates we've come up with to protect ourselves, but there's this unshakeable image of a ten-metre tsunami wall being totalled by a wave that flashes through my mind every time I'm hurtling through an underground tunnel in a metal tin.

Anyway, in this fragile state, the constipation-washing-powder advertisement struck a nerve. I sat bolt upright like an antelope startled by an unexpected rustle in the bush (or someone who thinks she might have just been groped), and formulated the well-worn thought, this time with unique clarity, that my life is wonderful. And that I really need to get my shit together, stop ruminating on done-and-dusted past events, and appreciate it. Maybe do some meditation and volunteering, read some Daisaku Ikeda, cultivate a bonsai, smile more. Stop being such a quintessential Tokyoite, yo-yoing from duty to destination with penitent expression, falling neatly asleep at every opportunity to show just how put-upon I am. And muttering English expletives, in my case, which has nothing to do with being a Tokyoite.

I've got it all, a perfect life – beautiful children, beautiful husband, beautiful apartment. I know it, and I know how

3

lucky I am. I know that any kind of whingeing is one major first-world sulk. From now on, I'm going to be happy, shut up all my demons and make everyone around me smile. I'm going to devote my whole life, all my energy to it, because it's the only acceptable thing, under the circumstances.

Given this impending turnaround, though, given that from now on it's going to be Ghibli theme tunes and freshly baked melon bread served with a smile, I'm just going to have one last scream before I start. A bit like consuming an entire bucket of Kentucky Fried Chicken the night before beginning the nattō and grated yam diet. One last gargantuan temper tantrum, throwing all my toys out of the pram and howling, and, after that, I'll be good forever.

2

Maybe this was when it began. On the Tuesday night when I was thinking of jumping off the balcony, while Tatsuya checked work emails on his phone.

I love the views from our balconies. We have a few around the apartment, which is on the thirty-second floor of a forty-storey block that looks like a giant game of Jenga mid-play. When we first moved here, looking down gave me vertigo, and, within the first week, Aki had managed to find a matchbox car small enough to push out of the tiny gap between the glass panels, leaving me dumb with horror, wondering if the anecdote about a penny thrown off the Eiffel Tower killing someone on the ground also applied to toy cars chucked off the thirty-second floor. Luckily, nobody was walking past so I haven't tested the physics, yet.

The terrace outside the sitting room is perfect for a cigarette; after the kids are in bed, I can close the blinds and sidle out of the glass doors so nobody can see me from inside. As if I've temporarily disappeared. In immediate view but far, far below, there's the Hotel Okura, its many gold-lit windows offering glimpses of businessmen and lovers, the topmost revealing an old-school ballroom with glittering chandeliers. If you look straight down, you can see the well-planned avenues lined with cherry blossom trees – shapeshifters innocently green until the magical moment in spring, when they suddenly explode into clouds of tulle. A highway pulses across the view like a neon artery, and beyond that the myriad skyscrapers form a constellation of lit windows in the city darkness, tens of thousands of people's lives, all with their intimate hopes and tics and favourite foods and difficult mothers-in-law. Closer to home, there are a couple of apartment blocks I can see right into and checking in on them night by night is like an ongoing mute soap opera. There's the family who favour morgue-style lighting in their kitchen, and the empty room further down, with a red leather sofa around the perimeter, a lamp always on. I think it must be an unpopular service flat, but Tatsuya is convinced it's the holding pen of a high-class brothel. Near the top, there's the apartment of interchangeable Westerners, forever showering and getting ready to go out, and below that the man in the suit who comes in late and haggard during the week, then sits out naked on his balcony on Sunday mornings.

I love that the roar of the traffic and the chattering voices (relative chatter, it has to be said – this is a very well-heeled neighbourhood and even on the ground people converse in hushed tones) dims to a comforting background swish this high up, almost like the sound of the sea. The stars feel so close and the ground so far away that I can kid myself I'm poised halfway between the two. The first drag of the cigarette, the cooling in my veins, the kick of an ice-cold

6

shōchū and the non-judgemental background breathing of the city. The relief of it.

On that particular Tuesday evening, Tatsuya was standing out on the terrace, ignoring the view and staring with furrowed brow at the blue light from his mobile, his thumb twitching. I, unusually, was around the corner on the balcony outside our bedroom, where Tatsu couldn't see me, and on that evening, just for a moment, I was straddling the railing. I only really thought this was a good idea for about one second, probably less. The millisecond my weight started to shift towards the leg that was over the edge, leaving the other dangling dangerously in mid-air, I threw all my weight back towards safety. No crackly-voiced Leo DiCaprio with a hand extended around here; the only person doing any heroic saving, even if it was only of my own sorry ass, was me. I landed in a heap on the floor, a sock hooked on the corner of the barrier keeping one leg suspended above me. My pulse was racing so fast my breath couldn't keep up, like anyone's would when the very real possibility of free-falling thirty-two floors onto a concrete pavement flashed in front of them. My head was sore where I'd thumped it on the floor. What. A. Twat.

I stayed in the heap, my pulse slowing; closed my eyes and listened to the unchanging sound of the highway. It doesn't seem right to find the sound of speeding cars so meditative. Truckers with shoals of fish from the coast and deliveries from satellite towns; families heading out for weekends away; commuters with their radios blasting and thoughts of home. Knowing that whether I'd jumped or not would have made no difference to the steady thrum of traffic brought a Zen-like peace which should probably have been derived from the breeze in a bamboo forest, not the dulcet tones of the Tokyo Expressway. Country folk would no doubt be horrified and consider my preferences as perverse as the ones that bankroll the Akihabara maid cafés, but despite my roots I'm a city girl through and through.

I opened my eyes and took in my proximity to the drain from which I'm convinced the cockroach we once found in the sitting room emerged. I've heard that at certain temperatures they can fly and given that Tokyo in summer is a furnace, one is permanently poised to gag. I scrambled to my feet, yanking my leg down and pulling something in my thigh in the process. Holding onto the glass barrier, now my safety net rather than my escape route, I crept like a crab towards the window to the bedroom, towards shōchū from the freezer and a bath.

As you can probably tell from the execution, I wouldn't say this was exactly a planned attempt. More a total shit fit that fortunately nobody saw, a physical manifestation of the screaming inside my head that sometimes gets so loud I want to drill a hole in my skull. The conversation that precipitated the nearly-end-of-my-life went like this:

'Tatsu, any chance you could give me a hand hanging up this washing?'

Tatsuya looked up momentarily from his phone, which he was examining while slumped on the sofa, sighed deeply, gave a noncommittal grunt and then returned to the screen. I returned to the washing, bristling with resentment. When neatly pinning a wet sheet got the better of me, I flung it on the floor and turned back to my husband. Just as I opened my mouth to speak, he shot me a look

8

that was a foul cocktail of feelings – irritation, pity, regret, resignation, contempt.

'Oh god,' he muttered, and escaped onto the good balcony, closing the door behind him.

And I decided to go throw myself off the other one, apparently. Or perhaps just to jump – 'throw myself off' sounds so overdramatic, as if jumping is a perfectly reasonable thing to do. I didn't really mean to; I meant just to leave and be somewhere Tatsuya wasn't, and leave the damn washing on the floor for him to find. Then I meant to pace up and down the other balcony and maybe smoke a cigarette, and then I started wishing he would come and apologise, or ask me if I was okay, which is never a good thing to think about because it's never going to happen, and even if it did I'd say something cutting and push him away, which brought a lump to my throat and a tear to my eye, etc. etc. And then the internal screaming got really bad. It would probably be fair to say that that evening highlighted the less than blissful working conditions in our marriage, and could arguably be named the prologue to the Kiyoshi situation.

I think 'less than blissful' is fair. I wouldn't go so far as to say 'hellish', or 'abusive' – well, sometimes it's hellish, but not because Tatsuya is any more badly behaved than the next Japanese salaryman. In fact, in terms of actual tot-uppable offences, he's a saint. He doesn't regularly drink to excess (occasionally, of course, but I'd like him considerably less if he didn't), he doesn't live for pachinko, he doesn't squander our money on fast cars, or even on hostesses, I'm pretty sure. He doesn't beat me; he doesn't have weird sexual proclivities and he's a loving father when he sees his kids. Which isn't all that frequently, but

9

what father does? And he's in good nick. If I didn't slightly hate him, I would definitely fancy him. So, there is no ear out there ready to be chewed off about my raging dissatisfaction with a man who slightly takes me for granted and could phrase things more pleasantly.

When I told Kiyoshi about the balcony incident, turning it into a hilarious, throwaway anecdote which didn't include the washing and demonstrated nothing more than my extreme spontaneity, he laughed his big open belly laugh, hitting the table in appreciation. But then he ran his hand over the back of his head through his short black hair, a habit he had when he was worried, or didn't know what to do, and reminded me, confusingly, of Aki. He put his hand over mine and squeezed. His hand was dry and warm, and he took a drag of his cigarette and started talking easily about something else, and I knew I didn't need to explain. I still catch myself thinking I have to tell him something, just to hear the way he'd turn a tragedy into a joke in a few true words, or for the satisfaction of hearing him laugh.

The tears were another sign that things in my marriage were somewhat awry. Unexplained over-emotion, like when Eri or Aki go insane over the fact they've put their shoes on the wrong feet, or dinner's been served on the wrong-coloured plate. When that happens, if my patience isn't already stretched so thin I have to go scream into a pillow, I drag the heaving little ball of tragedy onto my lap and try to find out what the real problem is. A less than understanding teacher at school? An argument with a friend? Anything a cuddle and a good night's sleep can't solve? I don't think cuddling would even have occurred to me if it hadn't been for Cassie and the Michaelsons; it isn't really a thing in Japanese families. My parents would smile at me fit to bust, pat me and jostle me, but nobody hugged me until, at sixteen, I had a fit of homesickness in New York one day during that first trip, and Mrs Michaelson folded me into a warm, perfumed embrace like it was no big deal. Even now the thought of somebody sympathetic giving me a cuddle makes me feel teary.

I wasn't much of a crier in the past. Things would happen that hurt like hell and I could just keep going, folding it all in and marching stoically on. Then there was a year or two after each of the children was born, when I felt as if whatever it was that separated me from the rest of the world had been ripped away, leaving all my surfaces completely porous. All the feelings in the world were in excruciating technicolour and I had no method of filtering them out. I cried at TV adverts and the children's first steps, at old people navigating the supermarket and pigeons wooing in Yoyogi Park. It was exhausting. Tatsu thought I'd lost my mind. Which I had, in a way, the older, steelier one, and had it replaced by an infinitely impressionable sponge. Luckily, time and sleep grew a little of the armour back, so that until just a year or so ago, I reacted appropriately to wildlife documentaries and photographs of other people's children.

But in those months before Kiyoshi . . . It is very difficult to run while crying, in my experience. I suppose it might not be as bad if you were crying outright, and able to breathe, but that swallowing-a-lump-in-your-throat thing, and trying to run, really doesn't work. There's a swanky glass-fronted gym at the bottom of our apartment building where the TVs on the treadmills have American channels on them, on account of the number of expats in the neighbourhood. I flick between CNN and MTV, trying to decide which is the more unrealistic and recently, disconcertingly, which is the least likely to make me start bawling. Do I feel more emotionally unstable about the plight of civilians in war-torn countries, or the transience of youth and time, dubiously represented by gyrating white people?

The last time I was overtaken by a crying jag, I remembered that I was using a pelvic floor weight in an effort not to end up incontinent, and had a vision of it falling out, sliding into my easy-dry leggings like a very small strap-on. Then I was simultaneously giggling and trying not to cry, which made me look and feel as if I were asphyxiating, and ended up falling in a tangle off the treadmill, a beet-root with bloodshot eyes. Fortunately, I was so sweaty the tears and snot and sweat blended together, and people just assumed I was about to have a heart attack on account of overexertion. Which is fine by me – clearly being thought of as incredibly unfit is preferable to being known as the insane weeping gym bunny.

That day, it was the Radwimps' 'Sparkle' video, from *Your Name*, that got me. That idea of having someone always beside you, that naive faith in a love that can transcend time and space. In my real life, I would scoff at the band's senseless name and the film's surreal body-swapping storyline, and argue that the idea of a 'soulmate' is both unrealistic and impractical. Not that I would ever admit to knowing the song, out of consideration for Eri and her embarrassment. But on a treadmill with headphones on, in that public but strangely private space, I choked back mystifyingly heartfelt sobs over Radwimps' cartoon teen-agers and Bump of Chicken and Ed Sheeran. When it was no longer physically possible to carry on with the running and gulping charade, I walked calmly to the sauna, where I listened to classical music for ten minutes and pretended it all never happened.

The logical conclusion would have been not to go to the gym any more, or at least not to watch MTV. But I, unfortunately, have never been one for acting logically. Even though it's a tendency that stays beneath a regulated interior, I'd say my true decision-making process mirrors that of an insane dog following his balls. I just happen to be fortunate enough to be sufficiently Japanese that the need to maintain appearances puts a tidy veneer on my animal instincts.

The veneer on our marriage is pretty shiny too. Tatsuya gets promoted regularly, I put home-cooked meals on the table and make sure the children are well-presented. Even Tatsuya's mother, with her sniffer dog's sense for anything that sidesteps upright conformity, has trouble putting her finger on exactly what it is about me that dissatisfies her. An aura that doesn't match with that of Tatsu's sister, who I like, incidentally, but whose interest in the quality of her homemade daifuku desserts is genuine. Unfortunately for my mother-in-law, her grandchildren are well-behaved(ish), my house is clean, and she can't persecute me for thought crimes. Yet.

3

Tatsuya and I have been together sixteen years. So long that the time is not far off when I'll be able to say, with pride or incredulity, that I've been with him over half my life. And I picked him so damn carefully. I know it's not attractive to boast, but really – it's not like there weren't other contenders. Maybe that's why I was so irritated, because I thought I'd picked a dud, made the wrong decision. There's a voice that whispers that it's inevitable after so long, after two kids and all the sleep we've lost and Japanese working hours, but I don't want to hear it. If I'd had a career, I could change jobs, apply for a promotion, *do* something. If I'd stayed in New York, I could have had it all, couldn't I? But I am a Japanese Housewife, a proper, old-school job for life, and you only get to choose your colleague once.

I thought I chose well – for over a decade, we went to bed together, had a chat before we fell asleep, spooned in the winter. You know, the little things. Now, when he's finished reading the paper, or half-watching the baseball while checking work emails, he heads to bed alone, his mind on brushing his teeth quickly, unsmiling, not seeing his own reflection in the mirror, and then throwing himself into bed, where I will find him lost, facing away from me with an arm flung above his head.

When it first got like this, I felt bad for him. Work in Tokyo is inhumane, and after Tatsu was promoted, his mind never left the office, and his body only rarely. The children have never known him any other way. I did all the things I was supposed to; waited up for him and cooked and didn't complain, sent him photographs when he missed the children's first laughs, first words, first steps. We'd talked about work before we were married, or at least I thought we had, but maybe it was actually a conversation about something else. He'd lamented that he'd barely known his father because he worked so hard, and envied me my father who was available, even if that was just because our home and his shop were one and the same, and I was always under my dad's feet. It was naive of me, to think that expressing your distaste for something means you can resist all the forces of family and society that propel you towards it.

I thought Tatsu would come back to us; I was even prepared to put up with the hours, if only when he was home it felt like he was actually here. But he didn't, and I began to run out of patience. All his energy was used up in the office, and what came home was a husk, a frowning stranger who used the flat like some kind of service apartment, volunteering speech only when something was out of line or we were getting in his way.

For a while it upset me so much that I thought I could shake him out of it. I used to follow him to bed or even wake him up when I got there, raging about the trail of mess he'd left behind him when all I'd done for the last fifteen hours was pick up after people a lot smaller than he was. Didn't he know that I'd been working just as hard as he had all day? The more sullen he grew, the harsher my voice would get, and he would look bored and grunt, and eventually start to second-guess me so all my dignity was gone, and it didn't make any difference anyway. And he never heard that what I was really saying was, 'I miss you, I need you, don't go and leave me alone.' And since he never heard it, I stopped saying it, and now I just clean the kitchen and have a fag and turn the other way when I go to bed.

All that shouting – it's done wonders for our relationship. It's *exactly* the method of communication everyone recommends for a functioning marriage.

I didn't set off on a course to destroy my good name (ha! Did I ever have one?) or my family's domestic bliss because MTV made me a bit teary or my husband was lax with the housework. But they were all indicators, I suppose, that trouble was brewing. They were the peeling paint and broken windowpanes of my home. Some houses can stay standing forever – there's a village near where I grew up where the entire population aged and died, and it's still sitting there in this valley, untouched for years. Typhoons and earthquakes, scorching summers and snow have ravaged the buildings, but on they stand. I could have done it too; gone on indefinitely without deciding to poise a wrecking ball above everything my life is made of. There's no defining reason for it in the creaks and cracks of my average housewife life. But then I met Kiyoshi. He's the reason.

4

I look directly at Laurence and try hard to focus on what he's saying, rather than the extraordinary colour of his eyes. They're green, and I know exactly how shocked my grandmother would be if she could see them. Obāchan never met Cassie Michaelson, but was very suspicious when I said her eyes were blue – what had she been eating, she wanted to know, to make them turn out like that?

Laurence and I are sitting in the glass-fronted bookshop café opposite Roppongi Hills, where I've been meeting clients a few times a week for the past eighteen months. My official title is Intercultural Consultant, otherwise known as tour guide to the alien land that is Japan. I got the job through my glamorous French friend, Eloise, who, despite having lived and worked in Tokyo for years, still assumed everyone around her was as straight-talking as they are in Paris and couldn't understand the constant miscommunications. When she recounted examples, the problem was blindingly obvious – she was hearing 'yes' when her Japanese friends and colleagues were saying 'no'. When we gaze into the middle distance and make sympathetic, affirmative-sounding noises, it means 'no'.

When we rephrase your question, or agree with your sentiment, it means 'no'. And most obviously, but apparently most perplexingly to Westerners, often the answer 'yes' – clearly, evidently, incontrovertibly – means 'no'. Eloise was so thrilled with these insights that she insisted on introducing me to her husband as the answer to his colleagues' relocation culture shock. My taking on the job was part of my push to practise my English again, and not go mad. I do try.

Now I have a relatively steady stream of clients eager to be told how not to offend the hell out of everybody (if in doubt, remove your shoes and put yourself down), and how to say a few useful things. Often, I end up taking the befuddled wives of American and English bigshots round the supermarkets, showing them how not to end up buying a cleaning product for dentures when they're after toothpaste, and what they can and can't eat raw. In the main, I like them. They remind me of New York, of how much easier it is to say what you mean in English, and the feeling of being on an adventure. The intervening years seem to have made me more and more Japanese, though, which I suppose is inevitable. Have Westerners always been this coarse, this chaotic? Does it really take a genius to observe, say, that nobody in this city raises their voice before 10 p.m., and that in public, and particularly on transport, it's preferable to whisper? That chewing gum in a temple is unlikely to ingratiate you to anybody? That nobody jaywalks? I don't know when I started sounding so much like my mother.

Laurence has some crucial advantages over the average Westerner; he is not overweight, and he listens to what people are saying. He's here on a secondment, doing a job that sounds surprisingly responsible given how laid-back and casually dressed he always is.

'So if I stand at the back of the elevator, everyone will think I'm arrogant?' Laurence is asking.

'Well, they'll probably let you off because you're a foreigner,' I concede. 'But if there's someone higher in rank than you, you should let them go in the back. And if you want to be polite, you should place yourself next to the numbers, and press them for all the people who come in.'

'Can't everyone just press the numbers themselves?' Laurence is incredulous.

'Obviously they can.' There is no point in explaining, because he will soon see for himself that in any lift he enters in all of Japan, that will never happen. There will always be a polite somebody taking silent orders from everyone who boards and pressing the numbers for them. 'But it's to protect the person of the highest rank, and to do the work for them. The highest-ranking person should always be furthest away from the door, so if enemy samurai come in, they will be furthest from danger.' I take a sip of my coffee. 'And you will be closest.'

'That's awesome,' says Laurence, charmed. 'The way that history affects how you stand in an elevator. And that there are rules about it. God, I love Japan.'

I feel the familiar mixture of pride in the unfathomable complexities of Japanese culture, and slight ennui at going through it with another amazed foreigner. Laurence, to be fair, seems normal, despite the ponytail at the nape of his neck, and his name, so unpronounceable on a Japanese tongue that there's the very real possibility people will avoid him just so they don't have to take it on. Loh-len-su? Roar-ren-su? Impossible. Like all foreigners, even though he's clean enough and appropriately dressed, there's too much of him, all over the place. Looking at his face, with its stylish stubble and double-hooded eyelids, and his earring, and his limbs which seem to spread out in all directions, and his backpack on the floor, can make my brain hurt, like trying to infer meaning from a Jackson Pollock painting.

Inoffensively, by Western standards, he takes a tissue out of his pocket and blows his nose. I consider telling him how unacceptable that is, but can't quite bring myself to, when he looks so cheerful. Everyone else in the world can seem like a mad scribble, and setting eyes on the sleek black hair and ironed shirt of the Japanese waitress feels like a cool drink of water. Straight lines, and peace.

'There are rules about everything,' I tell him. I don't add, You will never, ever know them all, or understand them, and even when you think you do and think you've been accepted, you will be an eternal outsider. I should know.

'Excuse me, I think you dropped this.' A man material-ises at our table proffering a credit card. Though foreigners can hurt my brain, too-neat androgynous Japanese men don't do it for me either. The impression this guy gives, from the cursory glance I throw him, is of something between the two. Well-built, broad-shouldered, strong features. He looks straight at me.

I give Laurence a quizzical look. 'Is it yours?'

'No, I don't think so.'

'I don't think it's ours,' I smile at the man. For all our politesse, there's no way to put 'thank you' at the end of that sentence in Japanese.

'My mistake.' He gives an almost imperceptible bow, more like a nod of the head to passing royalty than any movement of the waist, and goes to the counter to hand the card in. I turn back to Laurence.

That was the first time I met Kiyoshi.

I totally lose track of the time, because Laurence and I get into an involved discussion about old British television programmes. When I was in New York, Cassie and I used to watch all the British shows we could get our hands on, because Cassie was obsessed with the accents, and I found the swearing therapeutic and the vocabulary hilarious. 'What an absolute fucking farce,' I'd mutter to myself, 'It really is the dog's bollocks,' while Cassie tried out the incomprehensible tongue twisteries of Liverpudlian and Billy Connolly's Scottish, having mastered the Queen's English long ago. I have no idea if any of it is representative of how people speak in real life, but just as I'm beginning to grill Laurence about it, I notice that, as usual, I'm late, this time to collect Eri from her music class. I jump up to leave, and I'm cursing myself, and because I'm cursing myself, things aren't working, and I don't have any cash, and of course the café doesn't take cards. Because we live in Tokyo, the most gloriously modern-looking and backward-thinking city on the planet. 'They take cards in straw huts in Micronesia,' I hiss at Laurence, surprising myself, and him, with my vehemence. For some reason it makes him smile, and he regards me with friendly familiarity as he pays for me. I'm not sure why I'm reacting at all – even some McDonald's and Starbucks here are cash only. Having thanked Laurence, I try not to stomp out of the door, and spend an unfortunate few moments tugging at it until I notice it says 'push'.

'Here,' the man appears again and holds the door open. My cheeks flush and I want to stare at the floor. Instead I stare haughtily into his face. He is looking at me with an interest that suggests he didn't just engage with the social disaster I've created. I notice he's very good-looking.

'Thanks,' I tell him brusquely and stalk away.

I might never have thought of him again, because that week Eri had a piano recital out in the middle of nowhere, and a nervous breakdown to go with it, and Aki had a stomach bug and a nursery trip that I'd apparently agreed to go on in a moment of madness when the date seemed sufficiently far away not to count. In another, more peaceful, more mournful week, he may have surfaced because attractive men (or, rather, men who are attractive to me) are few and far between, and I sometimes like to dwell on them the way one might a beautiful view. As if I am an old, old lady, with my dancing days behind me. Which I am, effectively.

If I'd brought him to mind in an idle moment, I might have been pleased that he was age-appropriately attractive, not like Aki's football coaches who sometimes catch me out with their athleticism and confidence, then make me question my entire psychology because they are actual teenagers. But that week was hectic, and long enough to wipe him from my mind entirely. Or it would have been, if it hadn't rained during Tokyo Fashion Week.

5

Eri turned ten last year. Aki is four. They're both at school, now. I don't know how it happened. Back when they were tiny, sighing mothers of older children told me to appreciate it while it lasted, and I, starved of sleep, cursed them and their failure to recall anything practical that would actually help me. Now I don't want to admit that I can't for the life of me remember when they started sleeping through the night or eating solids, or that the crooning softness of their babyhoods really did disappear in the blink of an eye. Sometimes the days last forever, and still the weeks and months and years go whizzing unstoppably by.

Holding onto anything, the feel of their hands in mine, the solemn things they say, feels even more impossible when the children never, ever stop moving. In the entire decade that Eri's been around, sometimes I think I've only ever got a proper look at her when she's been asleep.

My baby girl, the weight of whose round cheeks I can still feel in the palm of my hand, and the ghost of whose huggable chubby self still fits in the crook of my elbow, now looks like a colt. A furious colt, to be precise. She isn't always furious – mainly she's shy, or thinking, and when she smiles it's like the sun came out, but the overall impression is of fury, and long limbs. She and her brother both have those almond-shaped eyes that seem to disappear when they look down, so you can't tell if they're avoiding eye contact or have in fact gone to sleep standing up, and that poreless skin that glows like copper the moment the sun so much as glances at it.

My own mother spent all my sun-drenched childhood summers underneath a black parasol, in a state of perpetual dismay at my failure to wear only beekeeper's costumes, preferably indoors, to maintain the paper white of my skin. According to her, my daring to swim in the sea and play on the beach during daylight hours meant my face was going to cave in like a mummy's as soon as I hit twenty. It's not that bad – I don't look like a porcelain doll, but I was never convinced that was a hugely desirable look anyway, and apparently neither is the rest of the world. I remember the first summer I spent with Cassie, marching out onto her roof terrace in the heat of the day armed with magazines and bottles of lotion, specifically to 'lay out', toasting ourselves evenly on both sides like grilled omochi skewers, the caress of the sun on my back and its liquid warmth on my eyelids, so all the world took on a summer orange glow, the desirability of tanned limbs skimmed by mini dresses and denim shorts.

My children, like me, run around in the sun and have the aspect of happy walnut peasants; energetic whirlwinds displacing everything in their paths. But now, without warning, Eri is slowing down and developing the disturbing look of someone who is about to become an adult. At ten! Observing my own daughter like a voyeur, I find myself thinking it's no wonder the beauty industry is obsessed with youth, with the fresh, innocent look of all the potential in the world, all the paths still untrodden, all the doors not yet opened.

Eri doesn't even think about unopened doors or the endless possibility of her future yet – her pensive expression is usually just her trying to remember her eight times table. Clearly, Eri is still a child. But she's in that in-between phase already where the idea of her upping and offing isn't quite as alien as I'd like it to be. To the outside world, too, she's a mirage – sometimes the tomboy child I know so well, yelling and fighting with her brother; sometimes, fleetingly, a ghost of her future self, a young woman.

Her school uniform, a standard, navy and white sailor-collared Japanese number, was almost unbearably adorable when she first put it on, aged six, with her huge red randoseru backpack and her little round navy sunhat. That damn randoseru cost more than the whole uniform put together, and had to be paid for in instalments – it's hand-crafted, waterproof, unbendable, presumably bullet-proof, so that in the event of Fujisan totally losing its shit and trying to do a Pompeii on Tokyo, or the ever-threatened 'big one' actually making its appearance and the entire city disappearing into a fissure in the ground, Eri can put her backpack over her head to keep her safe. I'm glad that the foolproof contingency plan is in place but alarmed every time I see her hoicking it tortoise-like to school, her skinny little legs stoically balancing its enormous weight on her back.

Despite the not inconsiderable (mandatory) down payments on the school-backpack-cum-natural disaster-shelter, Eri has recently started refusing to carry it, citing its undeniable lack of cool, and stowing her vast number of school files in a much less cumbersome, hot-pink cherry-patterned backpack made by some highly desirable brand and purchased for her by Tatsu's mother. So now if an earthquake causes the roof of her classroom to fall in, I can at least be comforted by the thought that my daughter looks trendy. The backpack jangles with a boggling collection of diamanté-studded shapes and gorillas in tiaras hanging from the zip, and as she carries it over one shoulder, it has the effect of making her walk differently, less like a happy-go-lucky child and more like the enigma that is a teenager. And suddenly – and this is one of those thoughts I don't think proper mothers have – the uniform, once so cute and innocent, occasionally reminds me of scores of Japanese schoolgirl-related horror films, or, worse, the kind of anime porn I sometimes spot men in suits reading on the Metro, as calmly as if they're reading Shibasaki's latest, without so much as an embarrassed glance up, even when the rush-hour squeeze means my head is practically buried in the filthy pages. If she were lumpen or had those bow legs so many girls have or looked like a potato, I don't think it would have even occurred to me. But my daughter is perfect. Not too tall, slim, straight legs, hair like a black silk curtain, peachy skin, perfectly even features that she's just started learning to turn into a mask, so that neither I nor Aki can work out what's going on behind them.

They're not constantly on my mind, these thoughts. They just sometimes slam into other, more pleasant thoughts when they're minding their own business, like wild animals that need to be wrestled back into their cages. On a couple of occasions, I've even thought about moving her to a school with either a really far-out uniform, or, preferably, no uniform at all, so that her entire education is based not on the merits of classroom facilities or pastoral care but on keeping my fleeting discombobulating thoughts at bay. I can just imagine that conversation with Tatsuya.

So my baby is on the cusp of becoming a hot teenager and, to be frank, that is shining a rather unkind light on my own haggard countenance. Since Eri was born, I've spent considerably less time staring into mirrors than I used to. It's not an activity you can multitask with, say, hanging up the washing or making obentō. Not that I was insufferably vain, only averagely so, but I do remember spending extended periods of time studying my face the way those street-corner diviners examine their cards, or the palm of your hand. As if just looking could give me an answer. Was I pretty? Could someone fall in love with me? What kind of future was I going to have? What would my obituary say? My face was a blank canvas. Nowadays, I often have to steel myself to forget my own appearance when we rush out of the house and I realise I don't look anything like I want to. Things aren't quite the same: there's an almost indiscernible sagging of the skin around my jaw – the faint beginnings of what are destined to become my father's jowls. The droopy-eyed look my mother has when she isn't concentrating. I used to be startled by the vigour of my reflection when I caught sight of it, the shine in my eyes, the glow of my skin, resolutely clear even after nights spent in smoke-filled bars, drinking till the early hours.

There were times during my misspent youth – sometimes months or even years on end – when I managed to be satisfied with every aspect of my appearance, and this happy accident filled me with a confidence and comfort in my own skin that I took entirely for granted. In hindsight, I was bloody gorgeous. I realise that's generally considered an indefensible thing to say, but I am just stating an objective fact. I can give you a list of my faults as long as my arm, and yours, with categories for sub-faults and spider diagrams of talents I don't possess and things I can't do. But it just so happens that, when I was younger, physical imperfection wasn't on that list. Luminous skin, straight nose, long eyelashes, all my angles and curves pleasing to the eye. Fortunately, all the other twisted knots of my personality kept me from enjoying it too much; I still managed to bemoan the fact that I was the wrong size (too fat, too thin, or somehow both), and looked like a pug, or an alien. It was only when I caught sight of myself accidentally that I was pleasantly surprised by the symmetry of what I saw.

I was a good flirt, too. Maybe that's bound up with being a good liar. I could take a deep breath and decide to emanate a desirable aura, make whoever it was look at me, walk a little differently and be sexy, or enigmatic, or lovely, or whatever it was that was required in the moment.

I love beautiful things, beautiful people, the magnetism of someone you can't take your eyes off. It used to be fun morphing into that person, tending to all the details that make the fantasy, but now I can't even imagine it. It isn't as if I've turned into Jabba the Hutt; physically I don't look all that different. But nothing about me is inviting or mysterious or alluring. And where would I be luring anyone to – a den full of Hello Kitty tea sets? When would I be giving the come-hither eyes – on my way back from the supermarket, on my pink mamachari bicycle, with bags of groceries loaded onto the front and back baskets?

In my anorak, dripping wet, at the door of Eri's ballet class with its distinct children's aroma of funky shoeboxes?

It isn't as if I spend my days gagging to go strut my stuff, or would ever exchange the gazes of deep love I occasionally catch Aki giving me for the pawing attentions of someone I've never met. But I think I assumed that one day I'd get round to cultivating it again. One day I'd remember to be both competent mother and radiant beauty. Tatsu would once again be prostrate at my feet and I'd be full of the serenity of Venus.

6

My entire relationship with Kiyoshi was based on a misconception, and that suited me just fine.

I wouldn't even have been there that evening if it hadn't been for Eloise. I met Eloise a few years ago, at a work do of Tatsu's at an Italian restaurant just near the Gonpachi's where that final scene in *Kill Bill* was filmed. The restaurant is high up, and you can gaze down on the gardens where Lucy Liu was scalped while you sip champagne.

The night I met Eloise, I was wearing a fantastic dress, a printed, off-the-shoulder number, and sky-high heels. I'd bought the dress because it reminded me of something I might have worn to do a gig back in the day; this one would have been perfect for a sultry number in some jazz festival, crooning into the mic. It sat in the wardrobe while I laughed at myself for forgetting that I didn't have the life to go with it any more, but the good thing about any kind of do in Tokyo, especially round here, is that you basically can't overdress. I've seen women in feathered ballgowns getting on the bus at three in the afternoon, and the standards of presentation required for the school run would be considered appropriate for weddings in other countries.

I still like dressing up, though find it a little depressing if I make the effort and Tatsu doesn't even look up from his emails.

I remember, too, that it was the first night out without my wedding ring. I'd removed it earlier in the afternoon to do the washing-up and then, out of irritation with Tatsu over some argument we had as we were leaving, I didn't put it back on. Afterwards, it sat on my bedside table for months, and he never noticed.

Anyway, that night, the outfit was a killer, and if none of the men noticed, the women did, and gave me smiles of approval. I found myself seated next to a French client's French wife.

'You look *in*-cred-*ee-buhl*,' she told me gleefully, and I could tell she was a bit secretly drunk as well. What had momentarily threatened to flatline into a night of Japanese businessmen turned into the best kind of Tokyo piss-up. Evenings that start with divine free wine are destined to go well; Eloise and I made friends with everybody, even Tatsu's sort-of boss, sitting next to me, who would normally have made me feel obliged to sit up a little straighter and ask after his children. Turned out he was way more fun when I was in charge of refilling his glass, and started telling me about his closet love of rock guitar, and how he practised in the middle of the night when he got home and everyone else was in bed.

Eloise was a total catch, captivating and gorgeous, and in a combination of her very good English and my pretty abysmal high-school French, made more fluent with alcohol, we giggled like schoolgirls who'd known each other forever. She had a nine-month-old baby, a full-time job, and no guilt complex. 'I hated being pregnant,' she

31

announced. 'When she was born, of course, I felt something very special, but when you go back to work it is the best. The *best*!'

We ditched the men and went on to a rooftop bar full of expensively debauched Caucasians, where Eloise filled me in on all the expat gossip – 'That lady over there? That is her gym instructor. He works at the American Club. I think her husband knows' – and then to a karaoke joint where we crashed the booth of a group of telecoms colleagues and sang heartfelt renditions of 'Koibito yo' ('Oh My Lover') with them. And then for another meal, seven hours after the first one, ramen and rice and more carbs, with a group of Maoris I have no memory of meeting. During the day I only ever see Japanese people; other nationalities seem to come out in the dark, like vampires and bats. We ended that night dancing with African drag queens in a place that was definitely a supermarket when I passed it on my bicycle the next day, and I was sure I must have dreamt the African drag queens, because where the hell could they exist during daylight hours in Japan?

It transpired a week later that I had made a solemn promise to Eloise to come out with her and her friends on the opening night of Tokyo Fashion Week. For one night only, the designer shops lining the leafy promenade of Omotesandō not only keep their doors open until late but serve free bubbly to those audacious enough to go in and drink it. Omotesandō, picturesque and glitzy at the worst of times, is decked up to the nines with light shows and makeshift catwalks, cocktail flairing stages and champagne bars, and the beautiful people of Tokyo – and, to be frank, there are a lot – walk the streets in all the clothes that look phenomenal on the catwalk and are entirely unsuited to real life. I was simultaneously up for it and unconvinced – my French isn't great and groups of lively Caucasian girls have the ability to make me feel prim and pale, a watercolour next to their effervescent pop art.

The fact that all my mamatomo, my Japanese mother friends, would as soon commit infanticide as go out at night without their children added an interesting psychological flavour to the invitation. But that night, after the children had obligingly gone to sleep, Tatsu's routine of checking his emails while flicking between baseball channels and yawning drove me sufficiently insane that I escaped to Omotesandō on a whim, answering a siren call from a different life. The group folded me in like the long-lost partygoer I am, and I came home the next morning just as Aki started making his first happy daylight squawks. We rarely see each other for the rest of the year and I don't even know if we could interact sober, but every October, on Tokyo Fashion Week Opening Night, I'm my most confident, fun, childless self, and they've never known me any other way.

And then, on my fourth Tokyo Fashion Week, a fortnight after I met Kiyoshi without realising, it rains for the first year ever. I'm wearing a dress that hugs every contour of my frame, with a back that scoops to only an inch or two above the top of my pants. I'd never wear it out alone, but with the French gang, and their unquestioning sexiness and raucous laughter, I'd feel like a prude in anything else. The rain is summer rain, monsoon rain, even though the season ended weeks before, like the Nile emptying over our heads, and refracting the lights of the avenue like floodlights in a diamond mine. Eloise is coming, she texts, she and Catherine are just necking their drinks at Giorgio

Armani, and they'll be at the Chanel next to Shu Uemura in a minute, where I should meet them. I'm standing under a little roof sticking out of a building near the station, admiring the choreographed precision with which translucent umbrellas shoot up as immaculate revellers make their way up from the Metro, and then shoot down again as their owners trip into Omotesandō Hills, which is decked out like the Academy Awards and swathed, this year, in thousands of pearlescent baubles. I turn my head to see if I can make out Chanel through the rain, and there he is.

Like me, he doesn't have an umbrella. He hurries the few steps from the station to shelter and runs his hands through his short mane of black hair to dry it. His eyes narrow slightly as they lock onto mine.

'You,' he says, almost accusingly.

'Me,' I agree conversationally. I'm struggling to place him.

'You don't have any cash,' he states.

'Probably not,' I agree, still mystified. Under normal circumstances I'd smile politely, vaguely, and walk away, but somehow the dress, and the rain, keep me rooted to the spot. The dress and the rain and something in his manner that's like a page I want to unfold.

'You don't know how to open doors,' he grins, and I remember. Confusion makes me momentarily awkward, so I raise one eyebrow in a challenge, like a thirteen-year-old who's just learnt what a double entendre is.

'I don't need to. There's always someone there to open them for me.'

He laughs appreciatively, his whole face transformed with mirth. The way he keeps his eyes on me makes me

34

feel enveloped in the joke, as if the contrast has been turned up on reality. 'Some mug like me?'

'I don't know if you're a mug.'

'No, you don't.' That's all he says, that short, innocuous phrase, but it takes him perhaps a beat longer than necessary, and he's looking at me as he says it. I notice again how good-looking he is.

'I'm waiting for my friend,' I say, turning my head to hide my thoughts.

'Does she have an umbrella?'

'Probably not.' I inch forwards to stand closer to the sheet of rain pelting from the overhang, where the air is cooler. 'She's French,' I offer, by way of explanation.

'They don't like umbrellas?'

'I just don't think they have the same religious attitude to them as we do here,' I say, nodding towards the Metro station's umbrella dance.

'Maybe it doesn't empty a river on their heads in France.'

'Or their hairdos aren't as delicate.'

We stand in silence for a moment; long enough for me to notice that he's so close I can feel the heat from his skin against my arm. Long enough for one of us to leave. I want to look at him, but we're both gazing out at the rain, at blurred headlights and the thrumming wall of water.

'She's going to be soaked,' he says, and triumph that he hasn't said anything to end our standing here together makes my heart jump.

'She won't care. She's been drinking free champagne for hours.' I turn and look at him, and the satisfaction of it is completely out of proportion with looking at a man I don't know and started talking to thirty seconds ago. He's wearing a white shirt, and in the darkness he seems spotlit, the line of his jaw a statement.

'Have you?'

'Not yet.'

'You're getting wet,' and he indicates my back with the tip of his fingers, as if he's about to brush the rain away.

If I'd just gone home with him then and there, maybe I could have saved myself a whole lot of hassle. The whole thing would have been over and done with in a couple of hours, and I'd have hurried out of whatever bed we were in and gone back to my life without knowing his name, or his number, or anything about him. Maybe.

Except that at that moment, I catch sight of Eloise hurrying along the pavement towards us. Her pace, and the jubilant energy in her wave, shakes me out of the dreamland I've stepped into. 'Here she is.'

Eloise is upon us in a moment, drunk and affectionate, grabbing my cheeks and covering me in kisses. 'Are you coming out with us too?' she demands happily of the man.

'I'm going the other way,' he says, and bows his head towards me again as he spins slowly on his heel to start walking in the opposite direction, his hands in his pockets. The plummeting feeling in my stomach makes me angry, and I turn back to Eloise, linking arms tightly and immediately entering into a nineteen-to-the-dozen chat.

Chanel is lit like the inside of a movie star's make-up box, a glow that makes everyone look flawless. Two champagne flutes down and I've convinced myself the encounter never took place, and the residual vertigo is just alcohol on an empty stomach.

'Mizuki!' Eloise has tried on a pair of red silk heels, with

36

hundreds of what may or may not be real diamonds on a strap that snakes its way round her ankles. 'You like?'

She's a pin-up girl for Parisians. She smiles so her dimples show and stalks around in front of the mirror with the delighted confidence of a child dressing up in its mother's clothes. The Chanel assistants are captivated and tilt their heads to examine her from different angles, making appreciative noises. Catherine appears from behind the mirror looking disdainful.

'We must go to eat,' she says reprovingly to Eloise in French. 'I'm so drunk I can hardly see. Melisande says she got a reservation at the yakitori place in half an hour.'

'Do you like my shoes?'

Catherine walks carefully round to the front of the mirror. 'You look like the wife of a whore.'

'That doesn't even make any sense!' Eloise objects. She examines the reflection of her perfect legs lovingly in the mirror. 'A very expensive whore,' she suggests.

'I must eat. Take the shoes off! And don't lose any diamonds or you'll be extradited.'

Woozily, Eloise unstraps her shoes, her slim, arched feet built for Cinderella doubles. She wobbles them back into her patent leather pumps, clutching my arm for support.

'Thank you,' she tells the assistants in careful Japanese. 'They're beautiful. But they're . . .' her limited vocabulary makes her give up on tact shamelessly, 'too expensive!'

The assistants nod regretfully, understandingly. Such a pity that such beautiful shoes should be quite so expensive.

'Now we go,' Eloise chatters happily to me, 'and eat yakitori, and swap to drinking beer.'

The rain has eased to a downward-travelling mist and the pavement is slick with the reflections of couture tripping towards more good times.

'I want an Asahi! Do you want an Asahi, Mizuki?' She's looking at me so earnestly as we step out of Chanel's sliding doors that I nearly walk straight into a man's very white-shirted front.

It's him again. I notice, face on, how big he is, built like a warrior.

Eloise has clutched my arm more tightly to stop us from toppling, a very real possibility without the added hazard of a man in our path.

'You should look where you're going,' she smiles at him, the Japanese in her French accent making it sound like a come-on. Backlit by Chanel, she seems only cheekbones and pillowy lips and Bambi eyes. I wait for the spotlight of his attention to shift.

'My fault,' he says with friendliness. 'I was looking for someone.'

Catherine comes stomping out holding Chanel goody bags and immediately starts trying to herd us down the street, complaining in furious French about her hunger.

'Get anything nice?' he asks me, before I can take a step to follow.

'One of everything.' The booze, and my own foolish, thankfully private, reaction, make me guarded and bolshy. 'Have a good night.' I start after the others. He comes too.

'I was wondering if I could take you out sometime.' It's a statement, more than a question.

I nearly stop walking but recover myself quickly enough to mask it.

'I don't think that's a good idea.'

'Why not?'

'Because . . .' The myriad reasons it is impossible for me to go out with him catch in my throat.

'Because?'

I can think of a thousand flippant, flirtatious answers that would only lead to more back and forth. Because I don't go out with strange men who walk into me in the street. Because I don't even know your name. Because my mother wouldn't approve.

'Because I have children,' I hear myself explaining instead.

'That's okay,' he says evenly.

'And their father.' It comes out in a rush because otherwise I won't say it at all, and still I can hear myself trying to fudge it, leave it vague, deliberately unclear. I force myself to be truthful. 'A husband. I have a husband. I'm married.'

His expression, which was one of benevolent interest, doesn't change, but the smiling lines around his eyes deepen a little. 'I understand.'

I will myself not to blush, but I can feel my cheeks radiating heat. 'So.' I state with aggressive finality. It doesn't cover up the embarrassment at all, of course.

'Well.' He stops walking, so that somehow I do, too. He reaches into his back pocket, and for one insane moment I think he's going to try to pay me for my time. Instead, he extracts his meishi, his business card, and offers it to me with both hands. He bows from the waist in a way that manages to be completely sincere, so that anyone seeing us would assume we were newly acquainted business colleagues, and also a giant piss-take. I'm not sure whether to be offended or laugh with him. 'If you ever change your mind,' he says.

I take the card, not with both hands, as I should, but like I'm extracting a ticket from a parking machine. I have nowhere to put it; Eloise has my bag.

'Thanks,' I say, and I walk away from him after the others, holding his meishi. The art of walking like a normal person seems to have deserted me, and it takes all my concentration not to walk like a robot, or break into a run, or, most importantly, turn around. I wonder if he's watching me.

7

A week later, I'm still pretending to myself that I'm not thinking about him. And in a way I'm not, specifically; I'm just overcome by daily brain-clouding attacks of lust. It's so not what's meant to be in the arsenal of an essentially middle-aged housewife engaged in risqué activities like grocery-shopping with her four-year-old. Aki is always thrilled to be sitting in the trolley and demonstrates his happiness by jigging up and down rhythmically, using the bag of tempura flour he's holding as a sort of baton.

As we pause in front of the tofu, an ancient lady stops her trolley to smile at him. Her face is basically one big wrinkle and when she smiles, it's clear she doesn't have many teeth at the top. Carefully, she leans forward to chuck his cheek and Aki, unusually, stops wriggling long enough to let her make contact before carrying on his dance.

'So energetic!' she marvels, her smile so huge her eyes have practically disappeared.

'And so noisy,' I add apologetically.

'That doesn't matter,' she assures me, patting my forearm. 'The most important thing is that he's a happy little boy.'

She shuffles on, still smiling to herself, each step of her

bowed legs careful. She is probably never going to have sex ever again, I find myself thinking. What the hell is wrong with me? She is a lovely, cosy, geriatric lady who stopped to talk to my four-year-old and I am thinking about sex. But another part of my brain is already calculating how many more years I've got before I'm as old as she is, and whether or not it's really going to be okay to spend them all being celibate, aside from giving Tatsu the occasional duty-shag. Many more decades and never another first kiss, or the thrill of someone's hand on your leg. Impossible thought.

At that moment, Aki whips his head around with huge urgency.

'Mama! There's Pokémon nattō! Can we get the Pokémon nattō? *Please*, I love Pokémon nattō so much.'

'Sure.'

'Mama, you are the best mummy in the whole entire world.'

I kiss his cheeks a hundred times as he tries to squirm away to get a better look, and try not to think about the fact that I'm really, really not.

8

I know that I'm not the best mummy in the world, because other women – and they don't even have to be mothers – are constantly wide-eyed at my parenting faux pas. Other mothers don't, for example, have to bring their baby home from lunch stark naked because they only packed one spare outfit and the baby managed to poo her way through it; or have the entire elevator system of their apartment block shut down so that maintenance men can rescue their child, who has somehow ended up alone in the lift and managed to jam the system. I don't understand why these things don't happen to other people. My mother tells me calmly that I've always been stubborn, as if that accounts for everything, which I really don't think it does. While I'm increasingly gung-ho about what people think – particularly the kind of neat, prim people in our neighbourhood with whom I have precisely nothing in common – it remains slightly disappointing, shall we say, that I'm far from getting top marks in something I've gone into all guns blazing. Parenting is savage – there is no other activity on earth that you could get up to do four times a night for two years straight, and at the end of it be merely in the running for mediocre.

It's unbelievable how binary parenthood was for me. Despite the lifetime of casually assuming I'd be a mother one day, and the nine-month build up to it, when I first held them both was still a lightning-bolt moment. When Aki was born, this slithery little alien, I saw the look of utter panic on his face and started to cry. The feeling that I'd made a terrible mistake was instantaneous – not because I didn't want him, but exactly the opposite. In that insane maternal way, I loved him so much, so quickly, that I didn't know what to do. It was immediately, blindingly obvious that there was nowhere near enough time in all my life and in all the world to give both him and his sister everything they needed and that I wanted to give them. The whole task was far beyond anything I was capable of, and the only possible outcome was failure of the most heartbreaking kind.

Everything was fine once I'd had some tea and okayu (proving, as I have long suspected, that there is literally nothing that can't be cured by that comforting savoury porridge), and Aki was dressed in a babygro and a little hat, his vulnerability at least slightly hidden. But that initial gut reaction has never quite left me. No matter how old Aki is, there'll always be moments when I think of him exactly as he was then, his black eyes wide open, apparently trying to look in two different directions at once to figure out what the hell just happened to him; his tiny little stick limbs uncertainly stretched out for the first time, bracing himself for who knows what. He was an actual part of my flesh that had been cocooned in safety and warmth and darkness and now found himself cold and exposed, blinking in the bright light. It seemed barbaric, and all I could do – then, now, ever – was hold him tight and try to make him feel like everything would be all right; more than that, make everything all right for him.

The whole overwhelming experience took me by surprise because when Eri was born six years earlier, she didn't look vulnerable so much as put-out and in charge, and my first reaction was to laugh. Pregnancy made me feel like I was a walking biology experiment – my main thought throughout labour was massive relief that this whole slightly revolting part of my life would be over soon and I could just be a normal human with children, not a semi-invalid with too many hospital appointments and carte blanche for medical professionals to ask inappropriate questions. Maybe it was this attitude that made my body, in its infinite wisdom, decide that what I needed was a complete overdose of bonding hormones as soon as the kids were born.

So, whether the initial firing shot was ultimately hormonal or not, I was thrown in full of zeal. Apparently not enough zeal, though – Japanese motherhood and its attendant housewifery is a cult, and its initiates take very poorly to anyone who thinks they can enter without going the whole hog. So even though I am a full-time mother with a cupboard full of obentō-making accessories, small details indicate cracks in my dedication for which true devotees would like to see me burnt at the stake.

For example, the fact that I was on occasion separated from the children for two or even three hours at a time before they were three, a holy time when mother and baby should be attached like limpets, doesn't paint me in a good light. Worse, the kids sleep in their own rooms, and I sleep in a bed with Tatsu, whereas by rights the marital sleeping arrangement should have ended as soon as Eri was born. Eri, Aki and I should be in one cosy pile and Tatsu should be off on a limb, or a sofa, by himself. Nowadays, I think that arrangement may well be preferable, but my naive decision has been made. Another option didn't even occur to me, tainted as I am by American lifestyle choices, and because in my childhood we all slept on the floor, negating the need for complex partitioning. I didn't realise it was that heinous a decision until I casually mentioned it to Ichiko, who has a daughter Aki's age, and she reacted as if I'd just told her I make the children sleep in kennels outside. In Tatsu's mother's eyes, I was a fallen woman by the time Eri was ten days old, when I decided that staying in our apartment (back then, a small one-bedroom place) any longer was going to result in insanity and the death of at least one family member, and had the audacity to *take a walk* with Eri slung to me like a small monkey. God (and all the well-to-do ladies in her seniors' Hawaiian hula-hooping class) knows what she thought when I took Eri to the park with Aki strapped to my front before he'd even been on this earth a week. Fortunately, by then I was even more immune to her opinion than I had been the first time round.

There have been periods when I've found myself submerged in motherhood for years at a time, lost myself willingly in the maze of my children's needs and triumphs. Then suddenly one day I come to, catch sight of myself in the mirror and think, *What was I doing again?*, in a way that's totally appropriate if you went into the sitting room to fetch something and had a distracting thought about an old lover, but not ideal if your reverie has lasted three years.

Sometimes, living in the world created by my children, knowing them better than I know myself but still finding them baffling, I feel like the rest of the world is nothing but shifting sands around me. I read somewhere that the twenty identifiable traits on the Hare psychopathy check-list apparently don't count in children, since they tend to display all of them. These include poor behavioural controls, irresponsibility, superficial charm, parasitic lifestyle, need for stimulation, lack of realistic long-term goals and impulsivity. I suppose it's unsurprising that one might question things sometimes, being in a state of indentured servitude to two small psychopaths.

9

I read in some parenting book that, ideally, your children's moods and behaviour shouldn't affect you too much, because if they do, you're giving them undue power – as well as screwing up your own life even more, presumably. You'll be surprised to know that this detached serenity is not something I have yet achieved. On a typical day, my emotions, along with the children's, will have gone through seventeen extreme permutations before we reach the school gates at 8.45 a.m. Take the morning after the Chanel encounter, for example. Aki insisted, as he does every morning, that he can get himself dressed. This means that everything's on back to front at best and not a single button is done up, but in the interests of everyone's eardrums, that's what he does. He hoists himself up onto his highchair in front of his miso soup looking so pleased with himself my heart contracts a little, and then asks me, 'Mama, I can get dressed by myself now – does that mean I'm a big boy?'

I tell him it does.

'But,' with the little crease between his eyebrows, 'even

when I'm big, can I still live with you? I don't want to live anywhere else.'

I assure him he can live with me forever, not bothering to mention the cast-iron guarantee that the moment he's big enough to live elsewhere, he'll be in such a rush to get out the door his shoes will be smoking.

The moment of sentimentality is short-lived, as simultaneously, Aki drops his soup in his lap and Eri storms in accusing me of hiding her school bag, which is clearly my favourite evening activity. By the time we finally get out of the door after a change of clothes, everyone is still hungry and Aki is in indignant tears because I tried to help him button up his shirt and dissuade him from taking his entire collection of tiny, losable Anpanman figurines to nursery with him. He's in a sufficient state that when the elevator arrives, containing a cluster of middle-aged men in suits, he has to be grappled in, and then makes weird growling noises and stamps his feet like the archetypal spoilt brat. The men in suits gaze noncommittally at the lit-up floor numbers above the door, while I wonder furiously why we have moved into a building designed for the sole purpose of causing me maximum embarrassment as soon as we leave the apartment.

The front lobby is cool and fragrant, polished shoes tap across the marble and Eri runs straight out into the street, ignoring my persistent instructions to greet the bank of receptionists by the door. They all stand up to bow as Aki and I pass, as if we're royalty, as opposed to aesthetic and social disasters. I try to bob and smile, drop all three of our bags and knock Aki over in the process, causing the receptionists to rush forward like a sea of impeccably dressed hens, fussing and picking things up. Eri is waiting

49

on the other side of the street for us to walk with her to the station, and I steer a disgruntled Aki across, only to feel him break free of my hand just as we reach the other side. I whirl around to see that he has run straight back into the middle of the street, into the path of an oncoming bus, which brakes violently. He hops uncertainly from one foot to another, then practically dives underneath the bus to retrieve one of his effing Anpanman figurines. I plunge after him, bellowing with rage and panic and then relief, which mostly just translates as rage, and doesn't come out in child-friendly language or earth-mother tones. The bus passengers tut their disapproval. I make my body language as obsequious as possible, given the iron grip I need to keep hold of a now howling Aki, as I pass the bus driver, who looks like he's been hit with a mallet.

Aki, remorseless, is impressively furious at being yelled at and manhandled and tries to make himself as rigid as possible, with the result that I end up fairly dragging him down the street. When we come to a level crossing, I realise that, as he hasn't done up his trousers, they have fallen down to his knees, and he's wearing his pants inside out and sideways, so they more resemble a thong than a pair of child's Y-fronts. I try to hurry him across the road so I can sort out his wardrobe on the other side, though this only leads to his screams, which have until now been torture-victim-siren-wails, articulating into, 'OOW! My HAND! My ARM! You're HURTING ME! Mama! Please don't HURT ME!'

At that moment, I notice some of his classmates and their families on their way to school, all their buttons and zips done up, holding hands and singing smiling songs to each other, until they are distracted by the horrifying spectacle that is me and my family.

My children. My life's work, my greatest loves, or-chestrators of total psychological trauma and everyday destruction.

IO

Despite all that, though, despite the emotional rollercoaster and the guilt and the rage and the sheer, headache-inducing noisiness of life with my children, there are moments, whole half-hours or even afternoons, in this life now, that are so perfect it takes all my concentration not to give in to melancholy and weep that it's passing even while it's still going on. There are Friday nights when, just as I'm about to fall asleep, I remember that tomorrow I can be with Aki and Eri all day long, and it's like the feeling I used to have before my birthday when I was small. Usually they choose those Saturdays to start the morning by screaming at each other, but the delicious anticipation persists.

One Saturday in late October, a fortnight after Chanel in the rain, Aki shakes me awake urgently because he needs to know if I know what the goldfish mermaid Ponyo's surname is. Eri is in a particularly buoyant mood and, while she's getting dressed, comes sashaying into the room wearing only her pants, with her skirt wrapped around her head like a headdress. She stands in front of the mirror admiring herself for a while before regaling us with a song from Aki's nursery about an acorn who makes friends with an eel, sung operatically. Aki is beside himself with delight, and Eri sashays out again with no explanation. She sticks her head back round the door a moment later.

'Can we go swimming today?' she asks.

'Okay,' I agree gamely. 'The pool in Ebisu?' The pool in Ebisu is enormous, and immaculate, because it chucks all the swimmers out once an hour so the guards can clean it for a full ten minutes. It is also plastered in anti-tattoo signs, which tickle or exasperate me, depending on which mood I'm in.

'We can actually go?' Eri looks surprised.

'Sure. After breakfast?'

'Yeesssssssss!' She goes whooping down the corridor as if she's won the lottery. 'Aki, we're going swimming! You can have the flamingo float.'

I'm smiling at them, enjoying an uncomplicated five seconds of parental love and self-congratulation, when I realise that Tatsu is also awake.

'Let's stay together,' he says, smiling.

I glance quickly at him. What is he talking about? Can he tell that I've been daydreaming about a stranger? 'What do you mean? Are we thinking of not staying together?'

He laughs at my reaction. 'Just, you know, in general. The kids are great. This is great. Let's stay together and carry this on.'

I don't know what to say, so I smile at him.

'You're happy today, Mizuki,' he says, poking me carefully with one finger, like he's forgotten how to touch me. 'I'm glad you're happy.'

That night, after we spend the day at the pool, Eri in her striped swimsuit with the bows at the shoulders and Aki so solemn with his armbands and rubber ring, his goggles pushing his cheeks out, I read Eri a chapter of Helen Keller, and Aki reads to me from his strangely touching tale of the small dinosaur who confuses a T-Rex for its mother. After I've kissed them both on their foreheads and their soft, soft cheeks, I go out onto the suicide balcony for a cigarette. A contemplative cigarette, this time, rather than a furious one.

I retrieve the meishi from the inside pocket of the clutch bag I'd had that evening, and after lighting my cigarette, I set it on fire from one corner. It burns more slowly than I'd imagined, then takes off, the glowing orange edged in grey devouring the fine calligraphy, until I pull my fingers away and the last sliver of white swoops upwards. There's no reason to burn it, apart from some streak of drama; Tatsu never looks through my things, and, if he did, a meishi would mean precisely nothing, changing hands all day, as they do, at the slightest opportunity.

There's another minor factor, which I don't let on even to myself as I smoke and observe the goings-on in skyscraper city, that the information I've just burnt to a cinder is branded on my memory. Teramoto Kiyoshi can be found at Kami, 5-12-8 Jingūmae, if ever I choose to seek him out. Which I won't, obviously.

11

I never really saw myself as the marrying type. Tatsuya is the one-night stand that has lasted sixteen years. We met at one of the last gigs I did, at a classy bar with a rooftop pool outside. It was late by the time he came in with a group of colleagues, in his suit, tieless. It's a look I've always been partial to. We locked eyes as soon as he walked in, and with his perfectly symmetrical face, his moody eyes, I knew exactly what kind of guy he was. I could just imagine his girlfriend, high maintenance, expensive, pouting and sighing while he effortlessly succeeded at everything in his life, looking chiselled and being a bit of a knob. I watched him the whole time I sang.

It was a surprise, then, when he found me after my set was over. He had such a sweet smile. I've realised in the decades since that it's because he must have had something to eat by then, and the anguished, enigmatic look he had when he first walked in, as if he were soldiering on through some dark night of the soul, merely meant that he was starving. Chances are he didn't even notice me when I thought we were having our thunderbolt moment, so consumed by hunger was he, although he swears he did.

'So, I enjoyed your set,' he said conversationally. 'How do you pick your songs?'

The way he was talking, I could have been his mate, or his mother, or someone he was babysitting. Flirting back was impossible. So I answered his question, and we talked about this and that, and he was funny and lovely and so incredibly hot – and so not interested at all. After a while, he went back to his colleagues without a backward glance, as if we were acquaintances who'd bumped into each other. I tried not to be too disappointed or wonder why he'd bothered coming to talk to me. I shared a beer with the drummer and watched the way he threw back his head when he laughed. You could tell he was popular with his colleagues. He gave each of that group of guys the same considered, good-natured attention he'd given me when we were talking, and didn't look in my direction at all.

After a while I gave up the ghost and went to fetch my things. When I came back to say goodbye to the band, their group had gone and only Tatsu was left, putting on his coat. When he saw me, he smiled, and I timed my exit so I could walk out with him.

The bar was in Shinjuku, and though places were closing, the streets were still full of people. We walked down dingy side streets talking about god knows what until I called it, and told him our routes were diverging.

'Or maybe you could come back to mine,' he suggested, so I did, although he was so completely unflirtatious I wasn't sure if he was inviting me back to ask me for my recipe for oden, or show me his stamp collection. He wasn't, it turns out, and, far from being the womaniser I'd had him pegged as, he was so guileless he opened a brand-new set of bedcovers he told me he'd only just bought and laid them happily on the bed. It has to be said that was the first and last time I've seen him do anything domestic.

The next day was just as uncomplicated – as I opened one slightly hungover eye, waiting for remorse or disappointment or something to come flooding in, all I was confronted with was the smell of Tatsu's shower gel, and him whistling as he put on his suit.

'Good morning,' he said cheerily. 'Did you sleep well? I was wondering if I could take you out to dinner this evening.'

He was basically a Care Bear trapped in the body of an underwear model. I was confused by him for months. Why was he so bad at flirting? Why did he do the things he said he was going to? Why was he so damn happy all the time? What was I missing?

I wasn't going to fall for him, obviously, because it was too much. Where was the bullshit, the mind-fuckery that made relationships so exciting, and traumatic? Tatsu was a good guy, but he was interesting, too. And weird, in his own straightforward way, and open-hearted and curious and generous. He wasn't artistically or existentially tortured; he had a good job in a software company and played a lot of sport and got on with his family, and approached life like it was a particularly enjoyable game. If it hadn't been for his beautiful face, he was the opposite of the kind of guy I would ever have got to know.

'I love you,' he told me after six months. 'You don't have to love me back; I'm just telling you how I feel.' Did he really say that? Could he have? We were married a year later, because I was finding out that I loved him more every day, and because I'm not stupid enough to think that if life throws you someone that good and you let it pass you by, it's going to let you hit the jackpot again.

12

Is it normal to fluctuate so quickly between feeling tender towards your husband and fervently wishing him a violent death? It's a few days after our swimming expedition, and in a sudden rush of goodwill, while cutting up a fruit salad for the kids' breakfast, I cut one up for Tatsu too, and just like Aki's, put the apple slices and grapes on top in the shape of a fox's face. My little man is entranced. The big one, in a different life, would at least have cracked a smile.

'Morning, Tatsu, I made you a fruit salad.'

'I don't have time for fruit salad, I have to go.' He doesn't look up from his phone.

'But I made it for you. Look.' I hate the petulance, the neediness in my voice. Especially in front of Eri, who stiffens, but doesn't look up.

He glances towards it impatiently. 'Mizuki, you know I don't eat breakfast. I always have coffee at the office.'

'I just thought it would be nice.' Why, oh why am I still talking?

'I have had coffee at the office every day for the past fifteen years.' His words are clipped, and he has gone back to his phone.

I look at him. If this were our first year, I would run a mile. If we'd been living together, or even married, but without children, this moment would be my exit cue. Who the hell is this guy?

Fortunately, there's nothing convenient to hand to hurl at his head. He walks out.

'Mama,' Aki coos. 'Look, I've made it so my fox is eating the orange. See? Can I have daddy's fox too?'

The fruit salad is still on my mind when Tatsu comes home that evening. I am kneeling by the drying rack folding and sorting washing, trying to remember if this is what I signed up for. There are girls out there who would love this. They would fold the corners of the towels over like a daring ankle peeping out beneath a dress, and make sure the potpourri in the entrance hall was always fresh. Why didn't he marry one of them? He comes in glued, again, to his phone. Tatsu with his emails and me with the laundry. Groundhog Day.

'I kept your dinner warm.' I will be civil. It never lasts long, this resolution of mine.

'I ate already.'

I take an exaggeratedly deep breath, which fails to keep my voice neutral. 'You could have told me.'

He sighs. 'I've had a really long day, Mizuki.'

'Don't put my name at the end of a sentence.' It reminds me of being told off by a headmaster. I know he knows I hate it, because I have a clear memory of him laughing at me about it, before.

'For god's sake.'

In order to leave the room, he steps over me as if I'm a sleeping dog in his way.

I spend the next five minutes with my forehead on the

pile of washing I'm trying to sort, like a supplicant prostrate to a laundry deity. Eventually, I get up and walk to
the bedroom, where Tatsuya is lying fully dressed on top
of the bed, reading a newspaper.

'Tatsu, I really need to talk to you.'

'Mm.'

'That involves you looking up from your newspaper.'

He sighs. Oh, what a sigh.

'Do we have to do this now?' Still not looking up.

'When would you suggest we do it? While the children
are eating their breakfast and you're running out the door?
During a work dinner with your boss? Would you like me
to wake you up in the middle of the night to try and have
this conversation?' I'm less than twenty seconds in and my
voice is already verging on shrill. It feels like someone is
standing on my windpipe.

'Well, what?' He looks up at me with hostile eyes.
When we first got together, and the decade following, I
never even knew he was capable of such an expression
and would have laughed if anyone had suggested he
would turn it on me. I would have quailed in the face
of it, before, but now I'm so used to it, and so resentful,
that it just makes me angrier. Anger doesn't render me
particularly articulate.

'You know what.' His stony expression makes it easier
to get the words out. 'I want us to have a conversation
about the fact our relationship has gone to shit.'

He flicks his eyes with boredom. 'Why do you have to
be so damn dramatic all the time?'

'I'm not being dramatic.' I can feel tears forming and
do my best to swallow them down. The sound of my
own voice, the stance I must have taken, clenching my

fists, reminds me of Aki, and the tears threaten to spill. 'I am not being dramatic. You make me feel like crap. You're always in a bad mood and you criticise me all the time. And you never even notice I'm here.' This sounds so pathetic that my anger redoubles. 'I feel like you think you're the only one who does any work. I work hard, all day long, just as hard as you do, and you make me feel like it's not worth anything. You have no idea.'

There are no words, in the face of his curled lip, to explain exactly what he has no idea about. No idea about the minutiae of his children's lives, no idea how lonely folding another clean shirt can feel. The tears have started to run down my face now, and I push the heels of my hands into my eyes. Tatsu doesn't even have the grace to look uncomfortable, let alone feign sympathy, and sits still, silent. I think about how once he would have had an arm immediately around me, looking into my face and trying to make me laugh, and cry harder.

'I'm sure you work really hard.' He manages to make it sound sarcastic without inflecting it at all, so it'd be impossible to prove in a court of law. 'I work really hard too.' He sits silently for ten beats or so, while I snort and sob with dignity into my jumper. 'Can I go now? I have stuff to do.'

The rage is like lightning, instantly illuminating everything with its own colour. I'm so bowled over by it I start laughing, my nose running, my eyes stinging. Japanese is insufficient for such apoplexy. 'You're such a shitbag, Tatsu,' I tell him in satisfying English. I know he hates it when I address him in English, a language he struggles to get his tongue around. 'You are such a. Fucking. Shitbag.'

'Great, thank you, Mizuki. Why do you always have to

be so unpleasant? Are you seriously getting this worked up about a fruit salad?' He laughs humourlessly.

'It is not. About. The salad.'

'I don't have time for this.' He gets up and walks out, remembering to take his paper with him.

I'm aware of the argument that Medea-style shrieking is hardly likely to win him over, but apart from the fact that at this juncture I don't give a shit whether or not Tatsuya finds my behaviour winsome, proponents of this view are gravely missing the point. Their suggested fix is to be the perfect wife; to endear myself to him so that he starts behaving like a loving husband again of his own accord, and then we can sail happily into the sunset together. Well, I do not fucking think so. You may notice that this method distinctly lacks the moment where the husband flagellates himself about what a total inadequate he's been for nearly a decade and returns to the wife on bloodied and bended knee. At best, it might include him realising he's been a bit remiss and looking sheepish. But that is not good enough. I don't want him back under those circumstances. At this point, I don't want him back at all.

Tatsu hasn't got the genetic make-up for contrition – he'd try to laugh it off, or jokily apologise while thinking I was making kind of a big deal out of nothing. No. I want him so consumed with remorse he can't sleep, which is perhaps why the sight of his peacefully sleeping back is a nightly source of aggravation to me.

But there are days when the flame of my anger is just about put out by a flood of sadness, and on those days, when he walks out, I crawl to the bathroom, where I can lock the door. I wouldn't want the kids to walk in and see me crying.

I think we've had this conversation twenty-five times in the last couple of years.

So I wanted revenge on Tatsu. Of course I did. Far more than the time I found out he'd slept with some client of his. To be honest, there was a massive part of me then that wanted to hear all the salacious details, but ultimately that didn't seem like the appropriate reaction. But this. He's made me invisible. With all the options I had, I chose him, chose him for life, for living, and he's frozen me out into an existence that isn't living at all. I'm in a cage without bars and I'm screaming but nobody can hear. I'm not even middle-aged yet and he's faded me into the background.

13

I stomp off to the balcony, and the sight of Tokyo glisten-
ing before me does nothing to subdue my fury. Frustration
makes me bang my fists down on the balcony railings. It
hurts. I turn back inside and march through the flat. In
an ideal world I wouldn't even stop to put my shoes on,
but I manage to step into them and grab my coat and
bag without breaking stride. I walk out, slamming the
door. The effect is somewhat nullified by the soft-closing
mechanism, which means it swings shut until the point
it reaches a bubble of air, then shudders closed almost
silently. Somehow, though all I've done is walk out of my
own front door, even the subdued lighting and carpet of
the corridor gives me pause. The larger part of me wants
to go running back inside our apartment to yell at Tatsu
some more, which would be a shit and pointless idea, so
I take the lift down to the lobby. I catch sight of myself
in the lift mirror and, even in my irritation, I'm thankful
for once that since I daren't pass the receptionists in the
morning without at least pretending to blend in with the
swanky residents of the rest of the building, I've inadvert-
ently come out looking presentable. The doors open, and

I pass the huge ornamental vases of flowers – maple leaves and red berries for autumn, now – and the night porter in his suit, who stands up and bows.

The outside world, which I inhabited only a few hours ago with my children, is now grown-up, illicit and full of shadows. Apart from my occasional forays with the French gang or work dinners with Tatsu, I've hardly been out in Tokyo after hours since Eri was born, my social interactions and occasional lone wanderings almost always taking place during the day. The mere fact of standing outside by myself in the dark is like slipping back into a garment that still fits me well, the city at night as welcoming as an old friend. The area is alive with the salarymen and women who have made their way down from the surrounding buildings, with the school's-out holiday spirits of the end of the working day. I start to walk down the road towards Roppongi, to walk out my rage in the hilly residential backstreets and eventually emerge tranquil into blaring noise and seedy neon, but halfway down the street, I realise I want to get away from Tatsu faster, and turn for the Metro. Down the tastefully lit banks of escalators, freshly polished this morning, through the station with its bakeries and artisan supermarkets, where I once dropped a bottle of red wine onto the pristine marble floor, causing social meltdown.

Everything is better already. There are other people, with other worries and other lives. I can blend into the Tokyo crowds, be nobody's wife, nobody's mother. It makes me feel calm to think I could melt into the relentless pulse of the city without anybody noticing, disappear like a trick of the light. If it were just me and Tatsu, I might have done that by now, be living a different existence serving drinks and smoking in a bar with disreputable clientele, only a kilometre or so away from where Tatsu may or may not have noticed that I wasn't, any more.

I ride to Shibuya, the obvious blockbuster choice of location. Sometimes it's all about the big bucks and starry lights. Outside the station, I'm immediately swept into a throng of people, past the information stand housed in an old train carriage, towards the three-way crossing. Buildings seem to disappear into the sky, restaurants and aquariums and offices and karaoke bars on every floor, a layer-cake of hidden worlds. Tonight it seems that every-one is young and shining bright, the huge screens above them and million neon signs rising up to battle any dark-ness the night might offer, and winning.

I stop for a moment, halfway across the road, looking up at Kyary Pamyu Pamyu, ten foot tall on one of the screens, performing a standard surreal candy-cane dance to heartfelt nonsense lyrics. I wonder if the rumours that she started her career as an underage model are true. All the shops are open and blaring noise; there is only sound, movement, colour everywhere I look, highlighted against the black of the night sky. The cars hold back for the party-going throng to cross, and it feels as if I'm standing at the centre of the world.

I meander up towards Spain Hill, past warrens of izakaya and their sellers standing outside with menus and deals, young men hustling as urgently for yakitori and beer as stockbrokers for shares. Past the arcades where girls not much older than Eri produce pictures of themselves looking like kinky Bambis festooned with love hearts, and crêpe stalls selling concoctions of strawberries and whipped cream the size of my head. Noodle bars, tapioca tea cafés, underwear boutiques, dessert restaurants, condom emporiums painted with smiling johnnies, until I am nothing but my sight and hearing and have no thoughts at all. Tokyo, if it doesn't provide an answer to my angst, at least has the effect of making me forget the question.

Gradually the psychedelic density of the shops begins to thin a little, and the buildings to shrink, until I find that I've walked to the backstreets of Omotesandō, and the more hyperactive shops have been replaced with wine bars and purveyors of French perfume, and commerce is on the first couple of floors instead of stretching infinitely into the sky. When I remember this journey, I ask myself if it's true that I was thinking of nothing and wandering easily along a route I'd taken so many times in my previous life as a child-free, night-crawling Tokyoite, or if I was doing something I'd been wanting to do since he gave me the meishi four weeks ago, that damned address guiding my movements as I pretended not to notice.

I keep up that sweet little lie right until the last moment, the moment when I can go, oh my goodness, fancy that, I appear to be at Jingūmae! Which fortunately for my pride is a busy and bustling place where you could legitimately just happen to be, without looking like a teenage fangirl outside a suburban house trying to make out you pass this way all the time. I start to have a word with myself, but an old me kicks in – one who wouldn't have had a second's hesitation in barrelling into a bar I knew contained an attractive man, and then making eyes at him until he bought me a drink and hung around for a month or two.

Kami is down a side street. I can figure that out surreptitiously enough, pretending to be looking at the names of the bars and restaurants on the main road while really checking out their numbers, and get halfway down the alleyway leading to it. It's silent and very dark; unbelievable that these quiet little houses exist ten metres away from the glitter of bourgeois Tokyo nightlife. Kami is beautiful, a traditional outer door made of slatted wood, through which you can see a stone path, raked white gravel on either side and minimalist shrubbery, lit up by paper lanterns guiding the way. The glow from the lanterns is golden, giving the impression of a portal to another time, a shimmering world of geisha and tradition. There's no way I'm walking in there, clearly.

I stop smartly and find myself looking around to see if anyone from the surrounding houses is watching me, which of course they aren't, since I'm not doing anything, and they have better things to do. I fumble in my bag for the cigarettes I've forgotten to purloin from their hiding place in my underwear drawer. I buy some from the vending machine on the corner, then march into the first bar I see, ducking through the cloth hangings obscuring the door.

As I walk in, a chorus of male voices bellows a welcome in my direction, and a shōchū is slammed down on the curved wooden counter almost before I have time to sit down. The place is buzzing, the waiting staff taut and energetic, all of them with a sense of ownership and purpose. And then – I would have had a drink, maybe two, smoked a couple of cigarettes, enjoyed watching the groups around me getting rowdier and admired the muscular spectacle of the guys hauling crates of beer from the basement. Eventually, I'd have taken the Metro home again, calmer, and climbed into bed with Tatsu facing the other way.

That's what would have happened if, just as I'd finished

my drink and was lighting my first cigarette, Kiyoshi hadn't appeared next to me at the counter.

'Can I get you another one?'

Thank god for cigarettes. Because the amount of time it takes me to finish my first inhalation and exhalation, like a carcinogenic meditation, is just enough for me to alter reality and erase the recent walk to his restaurant from my mind.

'Okay.' As if I'm just passing the time of day. He calls to the barman by name.

'Can I sit here?'

'Sure.' As if he's a stranger on a bus.

'Two shōchū.' He glances at my glass. 'With salted plums. Makoto, where's the lady's otōshi? Didn't they bring you anything?' Before I can answer, he tuts. 'Actually,' he calls to the cook, 'can we have a couple of skewers too? How's the liver today? The asparagus looked good.'

'Kashikomarimashita!' The cook practically salutes back, a foot soldier to his general. Kiyoshi, who's been standing, rests his weight on a stool and looks at me. His height barely changes. I take another drag of my cigarette so I can swallow without looking guilty.

'Do you always talk to waiters like that?'

His face creases into a smile and he looks like a boy. 'Only my waiters,' he replies.

'Your waiters?'

'Mm. They're good guys, usually.'

'Only men?'

'I have women too; they just tend to work in my other place. It's more refined.'

'Women don't always have to be refined,' I say, tapping my cigarette into the ashtray. I used to be a world-class flirt. It was my absolute favourite form of entertainment. Back in the day, I used to try it on with strangers for the sole purpose of keeping my hand in, like Holly Golightly practising kleptomania. And now I have the conversational skills of a cod.

'No,' he agrees cordially.

'What's your other place?' I ask him, just for something to say, as if I hadn't almost stepped right up to it and pressed my nose against the glass half an hour before.

'My other place' – the drinks arrive, and he slides mine down the counter with both hands like an offering, so it's right in front of me – 'is very nearly the place I always wanted.'

'Only very nearly?'

'I don't think anything can ever be quite as magnificent as what's going on in your head.'

'In general, or particularly in relation to places that you own?'

He smiles again, as he lifts his glass and taps it gently against mine.

'Kampai,' I nod.

'Maybe in general. But also particularly with places that I own.' He takes a sip, narrowing his eyes as he swills the liquid momentarily around his mouth and then puts the glass down, satisfied. I can practically hear the barman's sigh of relief.

'What's wrong with them?' I prompt, curious.

He looks thoughtful for a moment. 'I want them to feel as if you've entered a different place and left the outside world behind. And that's quite difficult to achieve.'

I take a sip of my drink. 'Sounds good. Although maybe the kind of ideal you might associate with a cult leader.

Or Walt Disney. I like this place, though,' I add hurriedly. 'And I bet your other one is great.' I sound like a dick.

'It's nice,' he concedes. 'You know, I don't even know your name.'

'Don't you?' Why am I playing weird and coquettish, like a bad black-and-white film actor? Why?

'Do you always talk in questions?'

'Maybe. I'm Mizuki.' I incline my head towards him in an approximation of the ironic bow he gave me when he handed me his card. I wonder if he remembers.

'I am Teramoto Kiyoshi. Hajimemashite.'

Hajimemashite. Let us begin.

14

The next morning is one of life's gifts – a morning after a night with almost no sleep, and still I wake up revitalised. Kiyoshi and I chatted our way through another couple of drinks, and somewhere between the second and third I forgot about being an appalling flirt and started talking like a normal human being. He made me laugh. Even better, I made him laugh too.

I'm sprinkling furikake onto Eri's rice, because she prefers that to onigiri, and using the nori cutter to make the seaweed on Aki's onigiri resemble a panda, and looking at their tightly packed, brightly coloured little bento boxes and thinking what a competent, brilliant mother I am. The children are slurping their miso soup when Tatsu sticks his head round the door to say goodbye.

'Did you sleep well?' I ask him breezily.

'Yes, thanks.' He looks caught off guard at the sight of his non-psychopathic and smiling wife.

'Will you be late back tonight?'

'Probably. I have a call.' For all his less than positive qualities, holding a grudge isn't really Tatsu's thing. 'Sorry.'

'No problem.' Having a functional marriage is easy, it

73

turns out. 'Have a lovely day!' I call after him as he leaves. You just have to pretend you're in an advertisement. I don't know why this didn't occur to me before.

We're nearly late for school, of course, because Eri can't find her kanji homework, but the ensuing accusations and wailing are water off a duck's back. In marvellous pathetic fallacy, the sun is shining as we skip down the street, and carrying Aki the last little bit because he claims to be too tired to walk is no effort at all. I'm somewhat mystified as to why I always try to make him walk, given how squidge-able he is.

'If I carry you, you have to hold on,' I tell him, so he puts his arms around my neck, his cheek pressed right up against mine. With his round yellow school hat perched on his head, he looks like a cartoon of the sun.

'Is it a trick so I'll cuddle you, Mama?'

'Ha! As if I need to trick you into it,' I retort, poking him under the ribs.

After I've dropped the kids off, I stop outside Aki's nursery for a few minutes to talk to some of the other mothers. Ichiko, a stolid woman who talks extraordinarily slowly and takes everything very seriously, is explaining how swapping the order of the ingredients while cooking steamed egg tofu makes it easier for babies to digest.

'We were just saying, Mizuki-san,' Ayaka says in an aside as the conversation moves on to the merits of the different rice brands, and whose husband prefers which, 'that it would be nice to set up a music class for the little ones.' Ayaka is dazzlingly well-organised and impeccably presented, and on any other day I would go home cursing myself that I wasn't more like her. Into a gap in the chatter, she asks, 'Didn't you used to be a singer?'

Before the official reaction, there's an infinitesimal moment of uncomfortable alertness, like animals disturbed while grazing. Ichiko blinks quickly, and then they recover themselves and there's a chorus of gasps and exclamations. I'm struggling to remember when I let this piece of information slip.

'Wow, how glamorous!' 'Mizuki-san I'm jealous!'

'Oh, it was so long ago,' I say, batting it away with a smile. For just a second, I imagine announcing that, as well as practically working in vice, last night I abandoned the children to stalk a stranger in a bar.

'Perhaps you could help us organise it? Do some presentations for the children?' Ayaka says, shifting the buggy in front of her, from the inside of which a shock-headed sumo wrestler eyes me with suspicion.

'If you don't mind how unprofessional it will be,' I demur. 'I'm sure Aki would love that.' He would – it's me who would hate it, making big actions with too much enthusiasm, like a children's television presenter, while everybody watches and coos. Hell on earth. And yet this morning, I don't mind at all, because it isn't all there is.

I fly around our usual supermarket, and since I'm feeling so damn energetic I pay a trip to National Azabu, the international supermarket in Hiroo, a luxury usually reserved for special occasions. It's fully Halloweenified, and the sight of the obscenely large orange pumpkins and imported balloons, and all the cheery Americans buying up candy for trick-or-treating, fills me with a disproportionate sense of wellbeing and cosiness.

I prepare an exceptionally ambitious dinner while humming along to the radio and then, when I've checked the apartment is immaculate, I go to the gym and leave bursting

75

with endorphins. I remember to take the kids a snack at pick-up, an unnecessarily expensive sweet-potato pie from Pompadour. My newfound friendship with a restaurateur has helped me see life itself in a whole different light. How unexpected that we should bump into each other quite so many times and get along so well. How refreshing to be getting to know someone new.

I'll tell you a couple of things about that first night that I knew, really, but pretended I didn't. The way he was the first person in years who thought about the answers to the questions I asked him and looked right at me when he replied. And the way I knew exactly where in my chest my heart was, every time he said my name.

15

While I always meant to become a mother, I didn't set out to become a housewife. I suppose that by the time I became a wife, a 家内, the kanji, reading 'inside (内) the house (家)', meant it was inevitable; that it was written, in fact. Especially since I now had a 主人, a husband, or a 'main (主) person (人)'. A protagonist in my life, and I wasn't it. Some days I can't quite work out how I got here; I plumped for the guy, I plumped for the kids, I just didn't realise that meant waving goodbye to everything else. Either way, my being with the kids full-time is the decision that's been made, and every year it continues, the less likely it becomes that there'll ever be a different one. Because what else am I fit for now? A calcified geriatric by Japanese employment standards, where even new graduates are considered too set in their ways to be the ideal employee. They like them fully malleable, contracted to the company with a binding signature in blood while they're still undergrads. My CV qualifies me for singing in the shower and not much else; no higher education and children, which means I have a binding post elsewhere. But once upon a time, before the children, before Tatsuya, I had a whole other life. Before I had domesticity in my title, I dreamt of my name in lights. The only reasonable reaction to that in my current life is abject embarrassment, but way back then, I really did.

The insane idea of becoming a singer would probably never have taken root in my well-behaved Japanese brain if I hadn't gone to New York when I was a teenager. If I hadn't gone to New York, let's be honest, a lot of outlandish ideas concerning my own freedom, equality and happiness would probably never have occurred to me and, arguably, I might have been happier and considered myself more free and more equal. Perhaps.

Going to America was my dad's idea. He was so proud of me, my dad; as impressed by my good grades in English as if I were excelling in neurosurgery. I'm an only child, and the reach of the life he wanted me to have bowls me over now, though at the time it was a given, or sometimes an inconvenience. My dad runs a sweet shop – ran a sweet shop, until genetic predisposition or unfeasible working hours killed him stone dead on his fiftieth birthday. Everyone liked my dad – you'd think they would, I guess, since he was the equivalent of the local crack dealer, but it wasn't just that. Even though he worked all the time, kneading and boiling and mixing in his big pans like a magician, ringing up the cash register or frowning over his accounts with his glasses perched on the end of his nose, he never looked like he was doing anything he didn't want to be doing. I always got the impression he was smiling his way through life, chatting to the children who came into the shop to spend their pocket money, making sure a generous gift was sent to his assistant Onō-kun's wife when she had a baby, and working nonstop was just the way he lived. He was always there – we lived above the

78

shop, and behind it, and whenever I wasn't at school my dad was only ever a paper screen away.

Since he died, and since having my kids, the questions I wish I could ask him are never-ending. I wonder now what decisions he made to keep our tiny family afloat, what inevitable sacrifices there were. Why a heart attack – was it just the make-up of his body and too much MSG, or was it because, secretly, it all stressed the hell out of him, being the sole breadwinner and the only one in charge? Did he want to give it all up and feel he couldn't? Did something happen? Nobody knows, and nobody can ask him. The grimness of death shocks me like a newly discovered horror every time I brush up against it, like the fresh confusion of a goldfish every time it reaches the edge of its bowl. It's only marginally easier now than it was back then to resist spending all my time and energy trying to find chinks in its armour, a hidden clause in its finality. I really wish my dad wasn't dead.

Anyway, before his untimely demise, my dad signed me up to a foreign exchange programme that meant I got to live in America for a year. I'd never even been to the airport before, a couple of hours' drive from the small town where we lived, and nobody in my family had ever boarded a plane. My dad had been to Tokyo once, as a young man, on the overnight coach. I never had.

To get to America, I flew alone to Tokyo, and then on to New York, where Cassie Michaelson and her family would pick me up from JFK airport. I remember the plastic smell of that first plane, crackling up the insides of my nostrils like I'd never smell anything else, and the roar of take-off. The night before, I'd been unable to eat, torn between excitement and wanting to call the whole thing off and hide under the kotatsu, safe between my parents. I didn't sleep a wink on the flight, watching movies play out on mute, feeling sick. I just wasn't very good at English – even Cassie Michaelson's name was a conundrum, that 's' so liable to come out as a 'sh' if I wasn't concentrating, the jumble of vowels in the second name, which was actually the Japanese first name.

My return ticket was booked for a year away. What if it was totally awful, and Cassie was horrible, and I was every bit as stupid as I thought and had to spend an entire year incapable of speech? Maybe I could get a job, and save up for a ticket home – except I couldn't, because I had to go to school, and I couldn't speak English. By the time I approached the arrivals gate at the airport, I was so keyed up I'd convinced myself I could stow away on the next plane back. But then there was Cassie, smiling at me and waving, and everything was all right after all.

New York was a revelation. Everything I'd suspected was missing from my sleepy hometown was there, glorious and dazzling, rushing past at speed. Cassie, in her cheery way, just assumed I was the same as her and folded me into her life, so I joined clubs for sports I'd never heard of, and a choir, and went bowling, and for pizza after school, as willing and as silent, initially, as an imaginary friend. Cassie's house was the size of the town hall, and I had my own bed in her room, with a pastel patchwork coverlet. It was stepping into a dream I didn't even know I had.

The English was hard, for the first couple of months, having to concentrate on what everybody said, translating the contribution I could make to the conversation just as it moved on. It wasn't just the language, it was the way they spoke; quickly, bitingly, and then laughing, all of it alien.

But only at first. Sweet, friendly and wholly self-absorbed, Cassie and her friends paid not the slightest attention to mistakes I made, in language or social niceties, and like the child of benignly neglectful parents, it didn't take long for me to grow in confidence.

I soon realised that the Michaelsons reacted with similar nonchalance when I did things that would have had my parents keeling over. The first time I came downstairs in an outfit Cassie and I had picked out at the mall, apparently suggesting I attend school in shorts that skimmed my bum by a centimetre, Mrs Michaelson merely smiled as she handed me a toasted bagel. 'That's a cute outfit, Mizuki.'

It wasn't that I hadn't worn shorts before, just that the lines that so clearly demarcated situations and places at home seemed to blur or disappear in New York. At school in Japan I could wear shorts to play sport, but only with my singlet and headband, and it had literally never occurred to me that you could do a maths lesson in anything other than a long-skirted school uniform. A teacher was a teacher and had to be respected – except here, sometimes, there were teachers you could call by their first names and flirt with. Cassie and I got drunk at a couple of house parties, and when her father came to pick us up his only comment was that he was glad we'd 'had fun and kept it under control'.

As far as I was concerned, Mr and Mrs Michaelson were like movie stars. Mrs Michaelson's job had something to do with the arts sector in New York City, and she often worked in her colourful home office full of silk-upholstered furniture, kissing Cassie absently on the head while she rummaged in her bag for the $20 Cassie needed, still on the phone to someone important. I don't think I ever knew what Mr Michaelson did (and I'm not convinced Cassie did either), but it didn't seem to stress him unduly, and he was always there at the weekends, teaching us to play tennis and shouting encouragement. He and Mrs Michaelson would go out for date nights, which meant Cassie and I could invite friends round and watch movies and eat popcorn on the gargantuan couches. Mrs Michaelson would kiss us goodbye, because she always kissed me too, right from the very first day, and she'd smell of peonies and look amazing, and Mr Michaelson would snake his arm around her waist and call her 'hon'. Cassie's eyes wouldn't leave the TV and it was all I could do not to ogle her parents walking out the door.

I was sixteen years old and clearly there were nuances of their relationship that were entirely lost on me. But god, I wanted that life. Even though I was just perceptive enough to realise that the fact my parents didn't casually kiss in public (and would have become social outcasts if they had) didn't mean they loved each other less, I still started to develop something like scorn for their traditional, proper partnership. What teenager wouldn't be seduced by the glamour of date night and silk upholsteries? The truth is, I still am.

I have no idea how my parents would have reacted if I'd come home drunk or paraded around in short shorts, because I never tried it. I went to America, discovered a whole other way of existing, and left home almost as soon as I got back.

It was the choir's fault. The school Cassie went to was fantastic, as far as I was concerned, but I'm not sure it was very academic. The lessons seemed to mostly consist of the girls writing each other long, involved notes with hearts over their 'i's and comparing nail polish shades and jewellery. Nobody seemed to mind very much about the considerable holes in whatever curriculum we were meant to be studying, but focused a lot more on the filler, a sort of *Glee*-flavoured gel, where the buzzwords were self-esteem and expression and happiness. There I was, my experience of the performing arts thus far playing sonatas at the town hall or singing the opening dirge with the rest of the school on National Foundation Day, and all of a sudden it was *Lights! Action! Make-up!*

And then there was the day Cassie was sick before the school winter gala, literally vomiting, with unexpected ingenuity, into her purse backstage just before we were meant to go on. In a panic it was decided I should sing her solo instead. She must have sung those verses hundreds of times in our room, and all I thought I was doing was pretending to be Cassie, pretending to be an all-singing, all-dancing cupcake, not the staid, quiet interloper I really was. But then I heard my own voice come back to me, part of the music made by these confident gaijin, and the entire audience bought my pretence. I was hooked, and the life I was meant to return to was totally screwed.

Screwed because I wasn't the daughter my parents had said goodbye to, and my hometown itched like a hair shirt. Screwed because I hadn't quite been keeping up with my kanji and Japanese studies, and when I got back – not unlike the protagonist of the folk story who comes back from the land under the sea to find that a hundred years have passed – I found that my one year abroad had been sufficient to turn me into a combination of village idiot and foreign weirdo. Messing up school is kind of a drag in

Japan, because it doesn't just mean you're not very good at science or you didn't do further maths – it means you can't read properly. Why, I raged at the time, did we have such a stupid, archaic system of letters when almost every other country on earth got by with the paltry twenty-six that I was now a master of manipulating? Shouting at my bewildered parents as if the Japanese alphabet (or three, actually) was their personal responsibility. It didn't take long for me to decide that my desultory attempts to catch up were going nowhere, and I didn't even care if I could read Japanese anyway. I was going to jack it all in and go back to New York to become a singer. Because it was that easy, obviously.

In my infinite adolescent wisdom, I didn't see fit to tell my parents what I was thinking, just stopped turning up at school and started earning money for my plane ticket instead. Without a single expense to worry about, saving was easy. I worked at the local convenience store, and as a waitress in the coffee shop in the station. I don't think I meant not to tell them; I was just so self-involved that it didn't occur to me. One afternoon my mother walked past the coffee shop and caught sight of me in my white apron. I hadn't known before that people's jaws could literally drop. I was so busy being tortured and wronged that I didn't even have the grace to react – just rolled my eyes and carried on pouring coffee. It's probably one of the reasons I fear Eri's adolescence; if there is any justice in the world, a massive comeuppance is coming my way. My mother wept that my morals had been corrupted by America, as she'd always known they would be, and I was going to get fat like a Westerner and be shot and never come home. It wasn't clear whether she was more concerned about the weight gain or the fatality.

I didn't know it then, but that was the last time my mother expressed an opinion about anything I said or did. In her eyes, once I'd gone back to America, I was an alien, someone she looked on with fond bemusement – and now my life in Tokyo with my fancy husband in the fancy apartment just compounds her view that I'm a stranger, a person who has nothing to do with the child she brought up. Sometimes I feel like I miss her, even when she's sitting right next to me. I didn't know I was pushing her away; it wasn't what I meant to do. On occasion, my whole life can feel like a pile-up of unintended consequences.

By the time I arrived in New York, Cassie had finished high school and was living in an apartment with some friends, attending drama school and existing on an allowance from her parents, topped up by the notes they pushed on her with good humour every time they came into town to take her out for dinner. She should have been insufferable, spoilt and sheltered, but she'd inherited her family's generosity and optimism and I lived on her sofa for months before graduating to my very own room and a share of the rent when one of the gang followed their dreams to LA. Cassie let me use her PC, and I spent my time looking up ways to become a singer. I trekked to weird locations to meet bands who turned out to be into psychedelic trance and went to auditions that purported to be for backing singers and turned seedy almost instantly. I was in so far over my head it was a joke, but, in that apartment, pursuing pipe dreams seemed normal, something you could discuss earnestly in your pyjamas over the sugary kids' cereal we ate for almost every meal, and with the stream of men we woke up to find beside us.

Eventually, between working at the bar under the apartment serving bad Mexican food and jugs of pink cocktails that tasted like pencil shavings, I got a gig singing covers in a severely underpopulated club, with a long-haired chain smoker on the piano. Glamorous it was not, but it was singing in New York. I started to get other gigs; a punter who may or may not have thought I would sleep with him out of gratitude put me in contact with a guy running an agency for wedding bands. I made friends with one of the bassists and ended up as their singer.

All of it was thrilling, like playing make-believe. Singing made me high. Every cliché that has ever been used to describe singing is true for me. When I sing, I'm free. It's like I've disappeared, and all there is is music, and I'm swimming in the current of every feeling I've ever had.

Little by little, I got better. The band got more gigs, better gigs, and I got more work off my own back too. I loved it all. I loved the rehearsals in cold, dank rooms, repeating phrases over and over until they were just a little better than they had been to start with. The nervousness of the day leading up to a gig, living my normal life, which to me was so exotic I sometimes found myself giggling alone with the wonder of it all. Making coffee, taking quesadilla orders from frenetic New Yorkers, then remembering with a jolt that I was going to throw myself off a precipice in the evening. The looks that would pass between the band during a set, figuring out how it was going, choreographing it by the seat of our pants depending on the mood, regardless of how much practice we'd done beforehand. Most of all the blinding light, so there's nothing you can see but white, nothing you can hear but your own erratic pulse until the expectant rhythmic tap on the snare. And then the music takes off like some winged creature beneath you and you're flying, navigating the cadences of the song, letting it soar and swoop, learning how to rein it in so it doesn't fly away altogether. When you finally land at the end, either a mad acrobatic dive following a loop-the-loop, or a snowy descent back onto solid ground, there's the half-second before there's any reaction from the audience that feels like a free fall. Then you hear the applause (you hope, though there were times, of course, in hard-bitten bars where barely a flicker would pass across the punters' faces) and there's giddy triumph, either enough to set off again or to keep you high for the rest of the night; the rest of the week if you're lucky. To me, there isn't anything like it. The fear, the ride, the elation. No wonder most musicians are dedicated drug-takers.

If my one year attending an American high school had been enough to put my hometown and me at odds, living in an apartment in New York was like blowing apart everything I was made of. In my whole life, I'd only ever seen a handful of gaijin at a distance, usually scientists who'd come to study the sand dunes our area was known for, and now I lived and worked and partied with a rainbow of nationalities. That people could be gay had never even occurred to me, and the first year I was there, Cassie and I spent weeks earnestly critiquing different costume choices for my colleague José and his boyfriend's dance troupe debut at Pride. Chris Rock and Tina Fey and all the other fast-talking, no-bullshit comedians and TV personalities became part of my lexicon, and as Cassie's English television fetish hadn't abated, so did Eddie Izzard and *This Life* and the wincingly accurate observations of po-faced Brits who made you laugh in the face of their grey depression.

I stayed in New York for three years and would have stayed longer, but finally, like someone coming to, I began to miss my parents. Cassie announced she was going to marry a hedge fund manager we'd agreed was a real drag the first time she slept with him accidentally. Also, I had an incurable craving for white rice with fermented soybeans and seaweed. And so I came back, but not to my parents. After landing in Osaka, I went home to check that everything was unchanged, then caught the overnight coach to Tokyo; the same one my father had taken all those years ago. Arriving in Ikebukuro at 5 a.m., tipped out onto the streets with the orange-haired hosts and hostesses, I remember feeling worldly-wise because of New York, a thousand steps away from the child who'd first stopped over in Narita airport a lifetime ago. But for sheer size and its ability to put you in your place, even New York can't compare to Tokyo. I realised my ant-in-a-colony status in about half an hour. Luckily it didn't take long to find a dorm bed in a suburban share-house where I could start again, armed this time with recordings and sets and some of the jargon, even if it was all in the wrong language.

I found work in Tokyo, eventually, built up my musical CV, the list of places both seedy and reputable where I'd belted out tunes. I could pay the rent, and say I was a singer without feeling like too much of a fraud. But the fact of the matter is that becoming a successful musician is like winning the lottery, and I just wasn't that good or that lucky. I was pretty good – people existed who followed my movements and cried when I sang (although that is also true of any number of singing chihuahuas on YouTube). But I was essentially a soulful showgirl, a puppet to other people's music. I can't write songs, can't even conceive of how you'd begin. No genius – eminently replaceable. For a while, there was work for me every night of the week; regular slots in reputable jazz bars, events, festivals, recordings on other people's CDs. But there wasn't anywhere else to go – nobody wants to make a covers album, and somehow I couldn't see myself joining Morning Musume's endless rotation of band members as the oldest by a decade. If I'd been a different person, I would have gone to music school, I guess, taught myself to write songs and taken on the Herculean and probably doomed task of steering my 'career' in another direction. Or been wily and flirtatious enough to get the movers and shakers, the entitled fat cats of the industry, to move things in another direction for me. But I wasn't, and I didn't.

There are things that are fine when you think you're on your way up. Things that I sort of loved when I started, because they meant I was opening the door to a world I'd thought might lock me out forever: the tacky sheen of cracked faux-leather banquettes, the stickiness of the floor, the cigarette smoke that meant my eyes were always red and a slight sore throat was par for the course. The lechers who found their way into every corner of the industry like a disease; the knowledge always that you were a commodity, and your shiny hair and nice skin and silhouette belonged to a lot of other people, but not wholly to you. The exhaustingly, unremittingly shit pay. Once it was clear that I'd reached the apogee of my own personal musical trajectory, that, Alice-like, first the top of my head and then my ear were jammed up against the glass ceiling with nowhere to go unless I worked out a way to shatter the whole structure through sheer force of will, the sleaze, the voyeurs, the grinding poverty lost a fair wattage of their shine.

And, finally, there were all those enlightening singing competitions on TV, which taught us that every second person and their granny feels that it's their destiny to belt out heartfelt pop ballads surrounded by spotlights and smoke, and eventually had the effect of making me feel foolish, as if I was expecting to get paid to eat chocolate, or some other activity enjoyed by millions and which anybody could do. So it wasn't that surprising to notice that I wasn't pushing as hard as I could when a gig was on the table, or that I was failing to make the vital proactive phone calls. Acting, as is my preferred manner, through inaction. You can hear this not very tragic tale and think several things – that I needed to be more resilient, more determined; that I needed to try it all out in a different place, a different country; to think outside the box and re-invent myself as an internet sensation. And, clearly, I could have done all those things, could have gone back to New York, maybe, but for reasons that I suppose are to do with meeting Tatsu, and with having come out of the hedon-istic madness of adolescence and found that in my genes I was a Japanese citizen, and with my relationship with my parents and god knows what, I couldn't, or wouldn't, and didn't. It probably wasn't a viable long-term career choice, anyway. What was I going to do, breast-feed between sets? Park the bassinet between the ashtrays and the amp and hope the baby wouldn't be deafened by feedback? It might have worked, until Tatsu's mother called social services. I wanted this life, wanted my children. I guess that, like with so many other things, I just didn't reckon on the fact that opening one door would mean closing another one so firmly. Perhaps my failure to fight for the music means I've forfeited the right to say I miss it, to claim that I ever loved it or that I wish things had turned out differently. But I do still feel all those things. I guess it was a divorce like any other.

The death of my singing dream kind of matters hugely to me, and also really doesn't matter at all. So, one person didn't get to keep mediocrely doing the thing they would have liked to do. Whoop-de-doo. There are 37 million of us in Tokyo alone – it has the effect of making it damn clear just how unimportant you are. Which is heartbreaking or relaxing, depending on how you look at it.

My old website still exists. I don't have the technical know-how to wipe it clean, so it's been doomed to some sort of digital purgatory, kicking around the dim and cluttered subconscious of the internet with all its other forgotten friends. I checked the other day, for the first time in over a decade, and there I am, informing you about ghost gigs and holding the mic, laughing. I look nearly the same as I do now, just happier. What an unforgivable thing to say, when my life now is the way it is. Maybe not happier exactly, just as if my edges haven't been so finely polished. Less demure, less taut. Freer.

16

The next time Kiyoshi and I meet, a week after the night in his bar, it's to visit a sweet shop in Kagurazaka. Kiyoshi took a while to believe me when I told him where I was born, and what my parents did. The province I come from is known for being the last one in Japan to get a Starbucks, and for having world-famous sand dunes, usually in that order. It's a place whose name you drop when you're making a point about how provincial someone is, or where you might joke about going on holiday, just so anywhere else you could go is glamorous in comparison.

'Mizuki,' he'd said patiently when I told him, that first night at his bar. 'Nobody actually comes from there.'

'That's rude,' I tell him in my home dialect. 'Just because I'm a country bumpkin, there's no need for you townsfolk to lord it over me.'

He is laughing so much he buries his head in the crook of his elbow on the countertop, the opposite of the stern boss he was when I walked in. 'How do you do that?'

'I'm not doing anything. I'm just talking.' I revert to Tokyo Japanese. 'You can't laugh that much at the way an entire province of people speaks! That's the way I spoke for years.'

'Sorry.' He's still snorting into the counter and when he looks up at me his face is open, as if we've just shared an intimate secret. Which we have, in a way.

'Do you believe me now?'

'I guess.'

My province is beautiful – or, at least, the countryside is. As well as a lack of global corporations and a plethora of sand, it boasts the smallest population of any county in Japan. Truly, a place of distinctions. And while in the town that translates to a need to concrete over the grassy open spaces that embarrassingly remind people of how un-derpopulated it is, in the countryside and along the coast it means land that's largely been left well alone. There's every kind of seaside, long stretches of white sandy beach and cliffs rising above the water, winding paths you follow down to the sea until you find yourself in an empty cove, nothing in front of you but a rocky stack with a single gnarled tree perched atop it, and the horizon.

Kiyoshi also didn't believe my dad ran a sweet shop.

'He did,' I assured him. 'It was tiny, all dark wood and so cold in the winter he always had chilblains.'

The house I grew up in was freezing too, as you'd expect from a building separated from the great outdoors by a paper screen and a twig.

'Do your parents still live there?'

'My mum. My dad died years ago. Not in the same house; with my dad's life insurance money, she got my uncle to knock it down and build one with central heating.'

The new house isn't as picturesque as the old one, funnily enough. I took Eri to that Edo museum on the

93

outskirts of Tokyo a while back, the one where they've collected up all the best-preserved traditional buildings from around Japan and stuck them together in a surreal, tumbleweed village. There was a shop front, decked out to look like an old-school grocer's, with a sliding door and baskets of goods in corners, and a single light hanging from the ceiling that did nothing whatsoever to dispel the darkness. In our shop, there were jars of sweets like pastel-coloured jewels catching the little light there was, and my dad with his apron and cap over his good clothes, rolling out sticks of rock. He and Onō-kun, his good-natured assistant, could put any design into the rock, and they'd roll out animals, faces, stars, messages, anything you could think of. On my birthday my dad would design one just for me, a treble clef the year I started piano lessons, a minute shortcake topped with strawberries and a single candle another. He never sold those ones, just handed them out free all day, telling anyone who came in that it was his daughter's birthday.

In the Edo museum, you could climb up from the dirt floor of the shop onto the tatami section behind, through the sliding screen that separated home from the shop. There was a kotatsu with a tea urn, just like there was at home, where I must have spent years of my life, doing homework, reading manga, huddling in the warmth and daydreaming. Removing my shoes in the genkan, stepping up onto the tatami in my socks, the old, cold smell of the house, all of it reminded me of why I left, of how I could love a place so much, and at the same time be choking to get out. Home felt like a sepia-tinted photograph that stayed still and tranquil while the rest of the technicolour world went roaring past. I'm glad that there's no empty shop in the squat little modern house my mum lives in now, and that she sleeps in a single bed, not looking at a space next to her where another futon should be rolled out.

I told a disbelieving Kiyoshi that there's a shop in Kagurazaka that still uses all the same equipment my dad used to use, and it was easy to agree when he demanded I show him.

'How have you never been here?' I ask incredulously as we make our way up the hill, past understated shops selling crockery and lacquerware. I'm wearing my secretly best clothes, my tightest jeans and boots that appear to have a heel as an afterthought but push everything up to all the right angles.

On the way here, after dropping the kids at school and meeting Laurence, I read my book and thought about other things, having convinced myself that this was more of a duty excursion than anything else, a trip that any self-respecting Tokyoite would take, to show corners of the city to people who didn't know better. When I stepped out of the station, though, and saw him standing there, also wearing jeans with a black jumper, smoking, looking relaxed, but waiting for me, I had to go back down a couple of steps to swallow the manic grin that was spreading across my face.

'I've only been here a couple of decades,' Kiyoshi laughs. 'And I've mainly been working. That isn't enough time to get to know Tokyo.'

As we climb further up the hill, the crockery in the shops goes from being crude, factory-made stuff, thick-rimmed bowls with uniform sakura patterns, to hand-thrown tea bowls painted with landscapes and koi carp, the type of

95

thing my grandmother would use in her tea ceremony classes. We pass a statuesque temple surrounded by a garden, its pagoda roof glittering in the sun. Kiyoshi stops to photograph the cluster of wooden ema plaques tied to the stand at the entrance. The plaques are painted with a snow monkey, and on the other side people have written their wishes and prayers.

'Are you meant to be photographing that? Isn't it like taking a photograph of somebody's diary?' I ask.

'I don't think they can complain when they've written them to hang up in public,' Kiyoshi says. He shows me the photo – the maple tree in the background is turning, its green leaves tinged with yellow and red. He flips one of the plaques over to make the point, and reads a message of love to Arashi, that boyband – now manband – quintet of coiffed, dyed hair, smooth torsos and even smoother chins.

'Huh.' The next one he reads is the same, and the next. Intrigued, I follow suit and we scan dozens of the hanging plaques, all of them dedicated to Arashi, wishing them well, declaring their loyalty and admiration.

'This is the temple of Arashi,' Kiyoshi states solemnly. The temple, ornate, ancient, composed behind its maple trees, gives nothing away. 'It is dedicated to diagonal fringes and female infatuation.'

'But how?' I want to know. 'Why isn't there a single ema about anything else? How can a bunch of crooners in feathers have commandeered an entire temple?' Japanese fans, I remember from my experiences on the lowest rungs of fame, are loyal and demonstrative to a fault, and there have been times when the question of whether or not one of Arashi's number is left-handed has been worthy of miles of newsprint. Still, a temple in central Tokyo seems a coup.

'Beats me,' says Kiyoshi, smiling. 'I love it.' After we have rung the bell, clapped our hands together and dropped some change into the enormous collection box below the bell pull, he goes to buy a plaque from the temple shop as a memento.

The paths by the temple leading off the main street are cobbled.

'Apparently there are still geisha around here,' I tell Kiyoshi in my role as tour guide.

'Yeah?' he lights up, then gets distracted. 'Wait, is that . . .?'

'Accordion music?'

'Yes.'

'Playing through the tannoy,' I explain. 'It's the French quarter too.' As well as the supposed geisha and tiny dead-end paths lined with topiary and lanterns, Kagurazaka is crowded with French-style bistros with chequered table-cloths and European wine bars. Kiyoshi starts to laugh.

'Do you reckon the cobbles were already here, so they thought they might as well make it the French quarter? Or did the first few French restaurants arrive before they decided to cobble the streets and pipe accordion music? I would love it if they played accordion music on the public tannoy in Paris.'

'Have you been to Paris?'

'I used to live there.'

Eri would be disappointed, I think, to hear that they don't play accordion music in the streets of Paris. It's the one place she's always wanted to go, it being the setting for some picturesque, unrealistic action-romance manga she watches with rabid concentration. I'm not entirely sure it's the most educational viewing for a ten-year-old but haven't had the heart to put her off it, as it's apparently what all the cool kids in her class are watching. I fear she's ripe for Paris syndrome, if ever she gets to see the city of lights.

Apparently, everything in Kagurazaka tickles Kiyoshi. He is enamoured by the cheese shop giving out samples of a Camembert the size of a bicycle wheel. He tries every single osenbei in the tiny wooden shack next door, where the crackers are baked over coals and soy sauce and sesame are painted on to suit your taste. The paper shop has always seemed to me like a treasure trove, with its beautifully patterned sheets, and boxes and chests of drawers and kites and notebooks made of origami in every imaginable shade, shot through with gold and silver, and he is the first person to have given an appropriately en-thusiastic response. He asks the charmed lady behind the counter where everything comes from, how it's made, who is making it. I turn over a paper wallet in my hands, appreciating the precision of the folds, its cheerful print, watching their interaction, enjoying her admiring him as he walks out of the door with me.

Hours pass before we eventually reach the sweet shop, tucked away behind a second, more modern temple, in be-tween an udon bar and a haberdashery. The shop front is a kaleidoscope of candy colours, presented every imaginable way – traditional paper boxes with compartments divided up into different patterned sweets, clear glass cubes full of round sweets with delicate lines of colour running around them like edible dolly's beach balls, spherical jars like bulbs filled with kompeitō, the rainbow-hued sweets that look like minute fireworks. Or teeny-tiny haemorrhoids, I find myself thinking. In the back, we can make out a man in a navy smock with a kitchen worker's cap, intent on his sugar dough. He stretches and pulls, stretches and pulls the bright pink substance into a pliable-looking tube before setting it aside.

'Irrashaimase!' he shouts, welcoming us in, before getting to work with the next colour, which will materialise out of what is currently a shallow vat of clear sugar liquid. Using a metal spatula, he scrapes it off the sides again and again, appearing to will it into solidity, until eventually the liquid yields, and allows itself to be picked up and folded. From where I'm standing, I can't make out his face, only the sure movements of his hands and an air of good-natured concentration. He reminds me so much of my father that I put a hand to my chest, like someone in one of the samurai melodramas my grandmother was addicted to.

'You okay?' Kiyoshi asks.

'Yes,' I say, embarrassed, hurriedly putting the hand down.

Later, after we've stood staring at the sweet-maker for an absurdly long time, the movements of his hands and the dancing colours mesmeric and absorbing; after we've bought and tasted the sweets he produced in front of us, fat little strawberry-flavoured discs with an extravagant bouquet running through them, we go for coffee in a place down a backstreet where I've occasionally gone to hide and read. We reach for the door at the same time and our hands brush against each other. The split second of contact sends a shock running up my arm, and I resolutely do not look at him as he holds the door open. As I step into the café, a minimalist, modern-Japanese place with unpainted walls and tiny alcoves containing flowers, I'm psyching myself up as if for an audition. It doesn't take long, a split-second decision – what I used to do before I stepped onto the stage and decided who I was going to be. Someone confident, smiley, uncomplicated, loveable. In other words, someone without a massive resemblance to myself.

'Well, thanks for showing me Kagurazaka, Yano-san,' Kiyoshi grins at me. 'That was the most fun I've had in ages.'

'Any time, Teramoto-san,' I smile. One beat of my heart is too loud, and I busy myself studying the coffee menu, pointing out the brilliant Japanglish in what may or may not be considered a series of racist jokes. Do they count if you belong to the race you're ripping into?

'So why is your life usually so un-fun?' I ask him, once the waitress has set our steaming cups of drip coffee before us. The smell is rich and enveloping, and it tastes like silk.

'Well, it's not un-fun, as such,' Kiyoshi says, leaning forward. 'This coffee is incredible.'

'Isn't it?'

'I'm getting you to make all the decisions in my life from now on. Where I go, what I eat, what I drink, everything.'

'Good idea. I think you will find things vastly improved.'

Kiyoshi laughs, a proper appreciative Santa rumble. Nice Japanese girls aren't meant to talk like that. I was supposed to look slightly flabbergasted, and maybe giggle with my hand over my mouth so as not to show my teeth.

'Well, what are you doing that isn't walking around buying up everything in Kagurazaka?' I prompt, before his laugh dies down.

'I set up my first izakaya eighteen years ago,' he explains. 'I was the chef, and the barman, and the only waiter.'

'It must have been very small.'

'It was – a counter with space for ten customers, underneath a cosplay store in Harajuku.'

'I've been there,' I suddenly remember. 'It doesn't have a sign outside. Next to that old record store that's been there forever. It's amazing.'

'Thanks,' says Kiyoshi, and just for a second he looks almost shy. I wonder what he was like as a boy.

'You weren't there, though,' I say now.

'I sold it, but only after it burnt down once and I had to start the whole thing again from scratch. Like my credit card bills weren't big enough already.'

He describes the string of places he's set up, working himself to the bone to get each one started, up before dawn to get to the food markets, prepping and cooking all day, serving all night. 'When I finally thought I had enough money saved, I started working on Gion. And it turned out I didn't really have anywhere near enough money at all. On opening night, I felt like I was sitting on a go-kart at the top of a hill and had started speeding down without any brakes. I was a mess. So tired I couldn't think straight and so broke it was a joke. I was sure it was going to shut down and I was going to have to go home and live with my dad.'

'Gion? *Gion*-Gion, in Ginza?' Gion is a glass and copper aquarium of beautiful people, known for being the site of Inoué-gate, when the married minister of finance was caught in a passionate embrace with the lead actress of the national 8 a.m. television serial, leading to her having to make a televised apology and him continuing as if nothing had happened.

'Yes.'

'You own Gion? So it didn't shut down.'

'No, it didn't shut down.'

It turns out that Kiyoshi has six places going in Tokyo at the moment.

'Six!' I don't bother to conceal my awe. 'How? Doesn't it get insane?'

Kiyoshi is chuckling at my reaction. 'I guess. I'm used to it. I have a lot of managers. It's good.'

'And what about Paris? When did you live there?'

'Before,' he says simply. 'That's where I learnt to cook.'

He speaks French, of course, as if owning six restaurants isn't enough. I sigh and wish I could speak French properly too.

'But you speak English,' he says, more a statement than a question. I tell him about the exchange, and Cassie.

'She was meant to come and stay in Japan for a year,' I remember. 'But thank god she ended up getting a place at a theatre school and decided she had to take that up instead.' I haven't thought about that for years, and imagine what a disaster it would have been if New York Cassie had had to share my one-tatami room with only a sliding screen between us and my parents, and be the only white person the town had ever seen. Perhaps it would have meant that I'd stayed at home and finished school. Without thinking, I find myself telling Kiyoshi about it, and then about the singing, with a little too much energy, because it's been so long since I spoke to anyone about it. There's so much to remember, and he listens with his whole body, nudging me for details and nodding like my memories are his own.

Even so, soon I'm embarrassed; even with the sarcasm and jokey caveats, it's not necessarily stuff I'd meant to tell him.

'What about your family?' I ask, in an attempt to change the subject. 'They must be really proud of you.'

'My mum died when I was nine,' he says. 'Cancer. I grew up with my brother and my dad.' He says it without any discomfort or self-pity and I, who have never known what reaction to give to bad news, find it natural to say nothing, and nod. 'Before she died home was so nice. It smelled of cooking and there was so much noise, me and my brother shouting and everyone talking and lots of family round all the time. We went a bit quiet after she died. My dad worked all the time so we were kagi-ko, letting ourselves into the empty house after school.' He toys with his cup, staring into it as if he's reading tea leaves. 'We never ate together because my dad got back so late, and my brother and I didn't know how to cook. I don't know what we were eating – rice and pickles, I think. Maybe cup noodles. Combini food.'

He sits back in his chair and I think he's done talking about it, but then he continues. 'Sometimes I think the restaurants are all just to get my mother back to the dinner table. Maybe not so much any more. But in that first izakaya, the tiny one, every time I looked up at the door there was a bit of me that kept hoping my mother would walk in.'

Even now, there are moments when I turn and expect to see my father standing there. Each time, I wonder when the feeling will finally fade away. Watching Kiyoshi, I suddenly realise it probably never will.

He squints at the spoon on his saucer, thinking. 'Some-times it felt like the part of me that my mother knew disappeared when she did. Because there wasn't anyone else who saw it, it just faded away.'

It's hard to remember who you are, without people who know you that way. 'I know,' I tell him, and he looks so rueful I almost reach across to touch him, before I re-member, and place my hand carefully on the table instead.

17

I'm a full two minutes late collecting Aki, and the other children are already long gone, their responsible, reliable mothers having stood outside the nursery door chatting pleasantly from ten minutes before pick-up. Aki is sitting on the carpet with his bag on his back, and turns towards me with a face of tragedy, as if I've left him unattended in a bin for eight hours, making me feel the full force of the one-hundred-and-twenty-second delay. His teacher smiles brightly, falsely, at me – she's had my number since the day I forgot his bento and sent him to school with a convenience-store sandwich. Once.

'Sorry!' I chirrup. I feel disoriented, as if I've watched several films in a row at the cinema and emerged to find it's still daylight.

'You left me,' Aki stutters, putting his hand in mine. I squeeze it.

'I didn't leave you, the bus got stuck in traffic.'

'Where did you go?'

'Out. I brought you a snack.' At the sound of the five magic words, all is forgiven.

Things with Kiyoshi didn't quite go to plan. I was going

to use him like a scratching post, just to see if I still had it, but I forgot to practise. I started off all right, but somewhere along the way I forgot which bit was pretending and which bit was me. It was easy to practise when I was younger, when I was a carefree girl about town, easy to captivate men just by not answering a question with a question. Stating your opinion is hussy-gold, subverting all their expectations so the dizzy confusion makes them see stars. They go, 'What do you want to do today?' and instead of replying with, 'What do I want to do today?', as if the question is far too deep to answer for yourself and letting them make the decision for you, you say, 'Hmm, I think I'd like to go for cocktails in that new bar at the top of the Aman.' It's so risqué they practically come on the spot. After that they'd be hooked, and it would be fun for a bit, but really it was too easy. It was easy to check out too, charmingly but firmly, leaving the fantasy intact so I could go home and get on with other things.

But when I tell Kiyoshi my opinion he just thinks about it and gives me his, and it doesn't count as flirting at all. And it seems that all I want is to talk to Kiyoshi; talk and talk and talk, before suddenly seeing the time and being jolted back to my real life and rushing off to pick up Aki. As we were leaving, he handed me the plaque from the temple in a matter-of-fact way. He'd bought too many other things anyway, he said. It was a token of his appreciation for me showing him around. The journey back made me think how much I used to hate lunch dates and the rest of the depressing afternoon that followed, back in my single days, when the timing of my various dates required serious thought. Not, of course, that today was a date.

18

Over the next few months we don't date quite a lot. Our meetings often coincide with days when I give Japanese lessons, so I go and legitimately sit in a café with Laurence first, doing my job, then almost coincidentally go on to meet another man. We visit a lot of places I know and that I think he'll like. Curating the city for him, I'm reminded of just how much I love Tokyo, its zebra stripe of neon and technology interspersed with dark, dingy noodle bars and age-old public baths.

I feel a ridiculous sense of proprietorship over neighbourhoods inhabited by thousands of other people, and an even more disproportionate sense of pride when Kiyoshi likes them, as if I invented them myself. We go walking through the cemetery in Nezu, our destination an ancient house so tumbledown it has a tree growing inside it, where we stop and have a cigarette and a tin of ice coffee from the vending machine standing next to it, like the tree is no big deal. 'We're in a Miyazaki movie,' Kiyoshi says appreciatively.

We go to watch taiyaki being made, the fish-shaped pastries filled with red beans, in the downtown neighbourhood of Monzen-Nakachō, and attend a service in a temple where people take their belongings to the holy fire to have the smoke wafted over them. One Sunday, when both the children are at friends' houses and Tatsu is mutely reading the paper, we admire the troupe of Elvis impersonators dancing with sincere abandon outside Yoyogi Park, and all the cosplay and J-pop dance practice going on inside.

'You never needed to go to New York,' Kiyoshi tells me seriously. 'You could have had a career singing *Sailor Moon* songs right here in this park. Imagine.'

As the weeks turn into months, I'm increasingly nice to Tatsu as I remember all his excellent qualities. Tatsu doesn't have a controlling bone in his body, which was one of the reasons we used to get on so well. The fact that in recent years this has mainly translated to disinterest is, it turns out, very convenient: as long as whatever I'm doing doesn't interfere with his life, he has no concern whatsoever about what it is, and once the kids are safely tucked up in bed, I'm free to do what I like. On the rare occasion he asks where I'm going, he is satisfied that I'm going to see Ichiko, the impassive, slow-talking mamatomo I have chosen as my cover because I know that if Tatsu ever crosses her path, which is highly unlikely, he will avoid talking to her for fear of expiring of old age before she reaches the end of a sentence. The fact that Tatsu accepts this without question is almost offensive. And yet in another way, it endears him to me. When we first met, he was the nice guy to my bitch, always mildly mystified by my distrust of everybody and anybody and the barbed comments that would come out of my mouth and leave me slightly ashamed. He'd laugh at me and ruffle my hair like I was a bad dog, and I'd think maybe there was hope for my eternal soul yet.

No such hope for Kiyoshi, who invites me to the opening of a friend's bar, which turns out to be a fetish club, staffed by PVC-clad dominatrices looking to cram you into a gimp suit and throw hot wax over you and more. Kiyoshi approaches the whole thing as he appears to approach everything, with straightforward enthusiasm and a not always wholesome glee, so it's sometimes hard to tell if he's taking the piss. He gets them to show him how to do up a gimp suit on another customer and is an attentive student to a dominatrix who teaches him about knots. The dominatrix is polite and conscientious and only slightly flirtatious. This is baffling to me, given their knot lesson means Kiyoshi's hands, which are strong but surprisingly dexterous, are almost constantly intertwined with hers. Just for a second, I imagine the feel of his skin, the pressure of his fingers, before I take a demure sip of my drink and concentrate too hard on the technicalities of the knots, like an attentive observer at an ikebana demonstration, a respectable distance between us as always. The dominatrix has the mannerisms of Eri's piano teacher, and Kiyoshi guffaws his way out of the bar, telling his friend that it looks fantastic but if he wants any customers he's going to have to find filthier staff.

We have yakitori in the night market in Ebisu and wander from bar to bar in the arches of Ginza. Kiyoshi talks to everybody, to the barmen and the chefs, but also to the taxi drivers and the men in suits and hard hats, waiting eight abreast with their white gloves and light-up batons to help us over pedestrian crossings where construction work is taking place. I can't believe I ever even whispered anything to myself about loneliness, when this is the city I've been living in all this time.

One night I take him back to the narrow, squalid streets of the Golden Gai, which I haven't had reason to frequent for over a decade. In the moment that we step into the maze of alleyways, I feel a surge of uncertainty, like knocking on the door of home but not knowing if anyone will be there. There are more tourists than I remember, peering uncertainly into the tiny bars with space for four people and aggressive signage turning away non-regulars. I lead Kiyoshi down one turning and then another, feigning nonchalance, and almost jump with relief when I hear my name being called from a doorway.

'Mizuki-chan!' Validation, in one word, that I haven't changed beyond recognition, and that I did live the life I imagined before. The glorious '-chan' at the end of my name, reserved for things that are young and cute.

Axel, self-named, with leopard-print hair and tattoos the length of his body that fuel the perpetual speculation about whether or not he is yakuza, hauls us into his bar and spends the evening regaling Kiyoshi with stories of the things the band and I did in our heyday. I'd forgotten some of them, and am pretty sure some of the taller stories are about someone else entirely, but I'm not about to tell Kiyoshi that. The bar is so minute our seats are pressed up against each other, and my awareness of the side of his leg against mine is like an electrical field I have to concentrate to ignore. The scent of him, oaky and clean, the tang of shaving foam and a mineral cologne that reminds me of the sea. I picture him showering, shaving carefully, appraising himself in the mirror.

'So she was good?' Kiyoshi confirms, nursing his drink.

'Mizuki-chan?' Axel asks with affection. 'The best. You're a lucky man.'

I start to stutter out a correction, but Kiyoshi doesn't say anything, just smiles a little wider then goes back to his drink, as if he thought of something he needed to consider, so I ask Axel about business.

Later, inevitably, Kiyoshi suggests karaoke. Of course he does; we live in Tokyo.

'I can't.'

'Why not? It used to be your job.'

'The way construction was your job, when you were a teenager.' The idea of a young Kiyoshi in the construction worker's baggy trousers, tapered at the ankle, is arresting. I imagine him with a bandana around his head, and a holster of tools, how strong he must have been. 'I'm not on at you to build me a house.'

'Why are you blushing?'

'I'm not blushing,' I say aggressively.

'I'll build you a house if you want. If you sing me a song, I'll build you a house.'

'I'm not singing you a song.'

He studies me for a while, his eyes narrowed. 'I just don't get it. You said you loved singing.'

'I did love singing.'

'You might still love it.'

'I do. I sing in the shower all the time.'

'I'll have to come listen then,' he says, one eyebrow rising a little. It's such an obvious retort it doesn't even count as a come-on. 'Karaoke is a national sport. Everyone does karaoke, even the guys at work who sing so out of tune it makes our ears bleed. Just do it already!'

I don't remember which gig was my last exactly, the

same way I don't remember the last bottle I ever gave the children, or the exact occasion when Tatsu and I last had sex. I feel like if I open my mouth to sing, if I take in that much breath and pour everything out, the only possible outcome is a world of trouble. Also, I've seen people do things off the cuff that have been amazing, and things that make me want to scrunch up my toes and die. Rarely does it lead to the romantic comedy moment of a meeting of souls, and if it did, the cheesiness of it all would mean I'd have to move to Hokkaido and live in an ice igloo for the rest of my life to get away from the mortification.

I purse my lips at Kiyoshi. 'Maybe,' I say. He's Japanese. He knows it means no.

It's a strange feeling, spending time with somebody who's succeeding in doing what they dreamt of doing, an impossible thing. I know how hard he must have had to bang his head against a brick wall, the staggering number of times he must have had to pick himself up after being thrown to the floor. His success story versus my pedestrian floundering and failing makes his efforts seem heroic, whereas in the end I started to believe that mine were just a bit embarrassing. I could be jealous, I suppose, that his dream is a reality and mine puttered out, but it's the opposite; he's proof that you can build castles in the sky, and I'm glad.

In these few months, it's hard to imagine that anyone in Tokyo is having a better time. We don't do a single compulsory boy–girl activity. We don't visit the aquarium and stand looking silently at the luminescent jellyfish in the official romantic spot; we don't visit a theme park where I can scream on the rollercoaster with my fingers curled up against my mouth, giving him an opportunity to put his arm around me, or laugh awkwardly. Since we're not dating, I don't wear date garb – pale pink and lace and pumps, like a strange cross between a vestal virgin and an office lady. I don't purchase a handbag that I have to hold in front of me like the English queen. We never have a meal where we don't say a thing to each other except at the end, to arrange another mute meeting. We smoke. We drink. We swear. I put a lot of questions into a particularly secure box in my mind where a lot of other shit is stored, and focus on the hedonistic pleasures of the moment. It's ideal.

19

I stare at the piece of paper that has just fallen out of one of Aki's jigsaw puzzles, wondering if I am now witnessing the apogee of maternal domestic OCD. In jolly writing illustrated with cartoons of happy mothers, the paper explains that all the pieces of the puzzle are numbered, and should one get lost, I can call a hotline and, for a fee, have the missing piece posted to me. I spend a moment digesting several fascinating facts – that someone, somewhere, has a job answering the missing puzzle-piece hotline; that some kind of board meeting convened and came to the conclusion that this was a logical thing to do, and that there are mothers out there so devoted to the order of their children's material possessions that they would work out the number of the missing piece, pick up the phone to call this hotline and read off their credit card number to rectify the problem. This last bit surprises me least. In an optimistic daze, I put the piece of paper in a file, ready for the day when I have finally morphed into the kind of woman who will sit down with a cup of coffee and attend to these things.

I head back into the kitchen, where the Co-op cata-logue is spread out on the table. Online grocery shopping, which had started in New York when I left, is not a thing here. To join the Co-op, I had to have an introductory face-to-face meeting with the delivery man, who spent an inordinate amount of time explaining the not enormously complex process of writing the number of things you re-quire in the correct order box, in pencil. The catalogue changes every week, featuring new smiling farmers and subtle variations on bento box staples, presumably to make sure everybody gets a turn. Having finished pencilling up our usual order for vegetables, fish and rice, I turn to the back of the catalogue, which sells non-food products and am tempted, as I am every week, to purchase a host of extras. Perhaps a full earthquake survival kit, complete with dehydrated food, foil blankets and portable toilets? While minor earthquakes are as common as rain show-ers, the fact that Tokyo is indisputably waiting for The Big One makes the idea of the survival kit not entirely laughable. It's not something I want to think about, and I turn the page. The star useless product this week features a woman who appears to be engaged in some kind of fetishistic ritual, with her mouth clamped around a large purple plastic object. On closer inspection, it turns out this is a device to exercise your mouth muscles, resulting, with dedicated use, in the reduction of wrinkles and fuller lips. Perhaps I could do my mouth exercises while wearing the Hannibal Lecter mask on the next page, designed to hold some sort of skin-bleaching kit in place. It might make Tatsu pay attention when he came to bed.

'Mamaaaaaa!' Aki's voice echoes from the toilet, which

he has been sitting on for the last ten minutes, swinging the door into the corridor open and shut. 'I'm finished!'

Aki cannot go with the door closed because, quite understandably, he is afraid of the toilet. No matter how many times we have demonstrated that all seat-warming, bidet and bottom-drying services have been turned off, he has never gotten over the time Tatsu pressed a button as a joke, so that on his entrance into the bathroom a contraption shot out from under the seat and sprayed water all over him. This is one of those things that in another family, and another life, we would have giggled over while cuddling him. In reality, I had a major sense of humour failure at yet another thing Tatsu had messed up for his own amusement.

I pad down the corridor.

'I'm not finished.'

I turn to walk away.

'Actually I am!' I'm torn between exasperation and contagious laughter, the grin spread across Aki's face as huge as if he's just invented candy floss. As I wipe my beloved son's bottom, I think for the seven hundredth time how deep motherly love must be. Tatsu has never been anywhere near the rear end of either of his children – the closest he came was when he handed me Eri, at about a week old, the whole back of her babygro fluorescent orange. The look of complete panic on his face was priceless.

'I want to see the poo, I want to see the poo, I want to see the poo,' Aki keeps up.

'All right, Aki. I said, all right.'

I drop the toilet paper carelessly and it falls on top of the poo. Aki, when he wriggles down off it, looks expectantly into the toilet bowl and then crumples, as if a puppeteer has cut his strings, in a heap on the corridor floor. His pants are still around his ankles.

'You put the paper in the wrong place!' he wails. 'You dropped it wrongly!'

You could not make it up. I literally don't have anything to say. I have a half-hearted dig around in my brain for an appropriate parenting strategy to deal with this, but can't quite bring myself to form the words, 'Oh dear, I know it's disappointing that Mama dropped the toilet paper so it covers your poo. It must be very frustrating.'

So instead I ignore him, flush away the offending evidence, wash my hands, examine my frown line in the mirror and neatly step over his bare bottom as I leave. This has the inevitable effect of making him howl even louder. Within minutes, he has worked himself up into a sufficient state that there are tears of fury running down his face and he is hiccoughing with sobs. When I come to pull up his trousers and give him a cuddle, he is outraged.

'Why are you laughing at me? I don't like people laughing at me!' In his temper, he is thrashing.

'Sorry, Aki-chan, I'm not laughing at you. I just thought it was a bit ridiculous that you got so cross over the poo.'

'I am not ridiculous!' He makes one final attempt to push me off, using his head as a battering ram, which has always been a preferred technique of his. It connects perfectly with the tip of my chin, making me bite down hard on my lip. Pain shoots down the centre of my body, and the metallic, salty taste of blood fills my mouth.

'Aki!' I roar, standing up and dropping him so he falls to the ground. Aki gives a piercing shriek which makes me feel as if my head is about to explode and I run to the bedroom and slam the door behind me. Blood drips onto the cream carpet. Emitting an actual growl of frustration, I head to the bathroom, leaving a trail of bloody spots behind me, like a murder victim.

In the time it takes me to stuff tissue into my bottom lip and wash my face, I've started to feel bad about Aki left howling on the other side of the bedroom door. I find him, and we make up. He ineptly aids me in cleaning the carpet, and then we do a jigsaw, from which I note with interest that a piece is missing.

Later, we go to collect Eri, and Aki and I get into an altercation about his ability to cross the road. I don't think that looking in one direction and then running across the street into the path of oncoming traffic is sufficiently cautious, whereas he vehemently disagrees.

'Hello, Eri-chan, did you have a nice day?' I ask Eri as she hurls herself out of the school gates like a dervish.

'Did you bring me something to eat? You forgot to put my gym kit in my bag! I had to sit out the class, again.' Her brow is down so low it's practically touching her nose. If it wasn't for the presence of her classmates around her, she would definitely have her lips out in the duck-pout I saw in prenatal photographs of her.

'Eri, you need to put your gym kit in your bag yourself. I wash it for you and put it back in your cupboard. We've talked about this already.'

'That's not fair.'

She stomps a few steps away, then stops and turns to me winningly, as if a cloud has unexpectedly been lifted. 'Mama, can Sayuri come over on Saturday?'

I hesitate, though I try not to. Sayuri is the devil incarnate, ten going on seventeen, a child who manages to patronise me and refuses to eat anything I cook. When Eri is with her, she giggles viciously with her hand over her mouth and defies everything I say with a wide-eyed stare and a sarcastic comment. I hate Sayuri. In the spirit of keeping Eri on side, however, and better the devil you know etc., I am about to acquiesce, when I remember something.

'Not this weekend, Eri. We're going to Kamakura to see the big Buddha, remember?'

'Uuuuurgh!' It strikes me with a disturbing jolt that this animal growl of irritation is exactly the sound I made when my lip was cut. I run my tongue over its tenderness. 'You never let me do anything I want!' She turns away, but not before I hear her muttering, 'I bet Papa would say yes.'

The evening continues in this vein until after supper, when Aki has thrown himself on the floor in protest because I've decreed that one ADHD-inducing sweet from his birthday party stash is enough. I sit at the table staring at my son, any sense of what may or may not be good parenting far behind me. Does it really matter if he has another sweet? Probably not. But to give in to someone who has gone purple with rage and stiff as a board over sugar doesn't seem a wise decision either.

I place my head carefully down on the table. Eri, who flounced away and slammed the door to her room over something I can no longer remember, has now started playing J-pop very loudly. At that moment, Tatsu, who never normally graces us with his presence before eleven, comes home. As I hear the click of the door, my spirits sink even lower. Hearing his father, Aki's yells subside to sad sobs.

'What's up, little man?' Tatsu croons, as Aki runs over

to hide his face in his legs. Swung off the ground by his father, Aki peeks out and gives me a sly but almost apologetic look from the safety of Tatsu's neck. He cups Tatsu's ear in his hands, still starfish baby hands, and whispers into it.

'Well, maybe Papa can get you another one,' Tatsu whispers conspiratorially back. Eri, hearing her father's voice, comes running out of her room.

'Papa!' She wraps her arms around his waist and gazes at him adoringly. With his offspring clinging to him like monkeys, Tatsu heads into the kitchen, but not before looking at me. It's not a look you could start a fight over. It's not massively contemptuous or full of hate. It's not massively anything, just the sort of blank look you might give the cat if it wandered in when you were in the middle of doing something else. He turns his attention back to his progeny, who are clamouring sweetly for his attention, giggling.

With all of my being, I want to punch his lights out.

20

I'd started listening to my self-acceptance tapes in the bath again, in the time before Tokyo Fashion Week, but by March, when Kiyoshi has been a regular feature for a few months, I've stopped. Therapy isn't really a thing in Tokyo; you do what you do, and if you really can't take it any more, you take the honourable way out and leave your shoes neatly paired at the edge of the bridge when you go. Cassie had a therapist, though, Cassie and all her friends, as if it were completely normal, to go for a dance class and walk the dog and then pay someone to listen to you for an hour, and in New York, where everyone talked so much and had such dramatic body language, it made perfect sense. I should ask Laurence if they do it in England too, whether it's a thing we repressed island nationers could make work for us. The idea appeals, but I just can't imagine it here. I'd go, 'I'm a mother with a husband who works hard and a nice apartment but I feel oddly dissatisfied,' and the therapist, who would inevitably be male, and older than me, would go, 'Well, that doesn't sound so bad. Have you considered getting a grip?'

Cassie listened to this online series of talks that she gave me the link to, and sometimes, when I need to hear a friendly voice, I listen to them and pretend I'm someone else, from somewhere far away. The woman who narrates them has the voice of a sex-line worker, slow and deep and dripping with emphasis, and there are bells and wave sounds in the background. All the talks are about accepting yourself as you are, being kind to yourself, seeing yourself as just one human out of many, doing your best, with as much right to be here as everybody else. I like the idea, and I find the talks relaxing, but if I think about it too much, the idea of self-acceptance jars. Some people, surely, are unacceptable, and the makers of the recordings don't know if I'm one of those people or not. How do they know if I phone my mother regularly, or separate my recycling, or keep my terrace free of furniture that could fly away in a typhoon, or tell the truth? You can accept yourself, here, but only if you're fulfilling your obligation to society. I guess that's why America is the land of the free, but we have lower crime rates and litter-free streets.

When I surprise myself with my more conservative Japanese views, I imagine sharing them with Cassie and can hear the disbelief in her voice. We kept in touch a good while after I came back to Japan but we haven't seen each other since I left New York, and now we just write at Christmas, when I look forward to the photo card and round-robin letter she sends. I examine them like a private detective, incredulous that we once shared a life, spent almost twenty-four hours a day together for years on end.

Sometimes I think that being friends with Cassie ruined any chance I had of being satisfied by a long-term relationship. We just had an untenable amount of fun together, so superior in our invincibility and our youth, unaware that our superiority only came from the fact we hadn't had time to fuck things up too much yet. It's head-bangingly obvious that no adult male trying to hold down a job and feed his family can be as unstintingly generous with time given to the analysis of events and feelings, as full of enthusiasm and energy and joie de vivre, or as fiercely, vocally loyal as a teenager living rent-free and attending improv classes.

The truth about my platonic Tokyo expeditions with Kiyoshi, obviously, is that I was out of my depth, and I knew it at the time, even though I refused to admit it to myself. You can shag someone no problem as long as all you see is their shell, and you show them yours, all painted pretty, and then you have some fun dinners and a few decent fucks and that's the end of that. But if you get to know somebody, and find out you laugh at the same things, and share strange tics; if it gets so good you only need to catch their eye to know what they're thinking, you are, it is blindingly clear, totally screwed. You're doomed to start an affair with a time limit on it, like life condensed. You have to lie around nursing an aching bosom and bleeding heart, and stop taking delight in anything, least of all being in the arms of your lover, on account of the fact you know it's cursed, and everything in your life takes on a grey sheen, like it's always drizzling, indoors. And who the hell wants to get involved in any of that? Least of all anyone who needs to grow their restaurant empire on the strength of their fizzing charisma and positive energy, or anyone who, rather more prosaically, really needs not to fuck up her children's lives.

That's why after a few non-dates, I had it nice and clear in my head that this was never going to be a thing. We would continue to hang out platonically, blamelessly, and life would continue to be immeasurably sweeter. I still didn't tell Tatsu about it because a) he wouldn't be interested and b) keeping secrets makes me feel safe. Having a secret makes me feel like nobody owns me, and that any opinion of me could always be inaccurate; no one has the whole picture, so it's like trying to judge somebody's appearance from a shard of broken mirror.

I like to have everything clear – even if the clarity is only in my head, and my decisions look fuzzy and badly thought-out to everybody else. They're not – they're just perfectly in keeping with my own logic, which probably doesn't correspond to yours. The way that to you, the burrow of some underground creature might look like a stinky mess of leaves and twigs, but to the creature, the layout is perfectly clear, and it's all meticulously arranged. You just need to understand the rules.

21

We go to Kamakura that weekend as planned, instead of spending it sucking up to Sayuri. We walk along the beach and visit the giant Buddha, and I spend some time gazing into that huge, tranquil face, hoping that some of that serenity and wisdom might rub off on me just by looking at it.

'Remember when we used to come here for the weekend?' I ask Tatsu, nudging him with my shoulder. Neither of us was any good at surfing, and it didn't make any sense, a sport that involved battling the ocean in order to have it carry you back to where you started from. It made even less sense that it was so much fun, and we would spend whole days being smacked in the face by waves, lying flat on our stomachs on the sand to recover and then plunging into the sea again. 'That time you called in sick so we could stay an extra night?'

My husband looks genuinely appalled and does a furtive glance around, presumably to check that his boss, fifty kilometres away, can't hear this admission.

'Yes,' he says, and he might be about to say something else, but Eri has found the shop selling Ghibli toys and demands all of his attention.

I suddenly remember another time we came here, one of the times lost in the fog of that first year of Aki's life, when my grip on the difference between dreaming and reality was tenuous to say the least. Tatsu had just received another promotion, a great honour that he accepted like a posting to Siberia, and we came for what was intended as a relaxing day trip to the beach, a sort of celebration of this double-edged turn of events. Aki's babyhood was entirely consistent with his character: full of enthusiasm and curiosity, he never slept, and was furious if he felt he was being excluded from anything. The exhaustion made me feel as if I'd been run over by a truck. Eri was still enraged that her position had been usurped by this tiny interloper and spent the majority of the time throwing tantrums or trying to get rid of the baby. The day was eating sand and noisy weeping because shells were hurting Eri's feet, and Tatsu, grey with fatigue, sat there twitching like a dictator corpse we'd somehow wrestled into leisure clothing. I remember tucking a gurgling, giggling Aki into his buggy at the end of the day and fighting back tears, hating myself. 'What?' Tatsu asked curtly. I was just another item on his long list of problems to solve.

Tatsu and the kids come out of the Totoro shop smiling shiftily, Eri clutching an appealingly fluffy Jiji, the witch Kiki's black cat with the red ribbon around its neck. She looks at me shyly and I'm so pleased she wanted something so childlike I squeeze her.

22

The first time Kiyoshi takes me to Kami, it's to help him woo somebody. Gion has plenty of foreign attention, of course, as the go-to place in Tokyo, and because it's the setting for that opening scene in *Manga Woman*. I tell Kiyoshi he should have refused on the grounds that *Manga Woman* is an asinine film with an asinine title and stars a blonde American in a role that was written for someone Japanese, for god's sake, and he says that while I'm world-class at my own PR, I should never get involved in anybody else's because I'd let too much ranting get in the way. This is exactly the kind of comment that would irritate the hell out of me if he were my husband or lover, but as he's fortunate enough to be neither, I find it flattering that he knows me so well. His PR, despite questionable film choices, is doing spectacularly well; I see Kami, much to my irritation, on *Terrace House* weeks before I set foot inside it.

'I have some people coming over who might want me to open a restaurant in New York,' he tells me abruptly one morning, when we're sampling the dango in the backstreets of Asakusa.

'That's really cool – mm, have you tried this sauce? Shit, I think I burnt my tongue.'

'In one of the new World Trade Center buildings.'

I swallow. 'Kiyoshi, that's fantastic news. Congratu-lations!'

'Mizuki. First of all, don't sound like you're taking the piss out of me. Secondly, it's about a million miles from decided, yet.'

'I'm not taking the piss out of you.' And I'm not, really, it just started when he took the piss out of himself, for being such a glamour whore and not setting up soup kitch-ens or canteens in third world countries, and it's an easier persona for me than being perpetually in awe.

'Anyway, these people are going to come over and check out Gion and check out Kami, and then we have to have a meeting that has to pretend to be a dinner with mates, not an audition for squillions of yen.'

I am licking the last of the mitarashi sauce off my fingers. 'That sounds stressful,' I tell him cheerfully. I love being able to tell him exactly what I'm thinking. Not having to put it through the good-parenting filter I use for my children, or the perpetual war communication calculations I do with Tatsu, or the edited, rose-tinted truth I feed my mother. Kiyoshi sighs.

'So, will you come?'

I stop mid-lick, like a cat surprised by its own reflection in a window. 'Me? I don't know anything about Kami. I've never even been there.'

'You don't need to know anything. You speak English. You scrub up nice. You just have to charm them.'

'Who else is going to be there?' I ask suspiciously.

'Some friends. Some people pretending to be friends

who are really part of the business – you know, Yoriko and Ryo and Sotaro, those kind of guys.' His PR, and his business manager, and the manager of Gion. His entourage.

'Ooh,' I nearly say in a silly voice, 'so I get to meet your friends now!' But I don't, obviously, because I don't always tell him exactly what I'm thinking.

'Lots of people?' I ask instead.

'Yes.'

'Nobody will notice me?'

'No. Nobody will notice you.'

'How would you explain me, anyway?'

He gives me a strange look. 'What? I'd explain that you're my friend.'

I feel like such an idiot that I'm compelled to change the subject, which Kiyoshi takes as acceptance of his interesting or stressful invitation.

23

'Ma-maaaaaaa!' Aki is shouting at me with urgency from his bedroom.

'Yes, Aki?'

The response is out of my mouth before I'm even awake. My heart is racing from having been rudely awakened from such a deep sleep, and the wisps of a dream float at the edges of my awareness like smoke. I've been dreaming of earthquakes recently, of our building, designed as it is like a pendulum, to sway but not to break, leaning so near to the ground that I, holding the children, am in an agony of indecision as to whether we should stay in the building or jump off, braving the distance. Now, as if the dream has spilled over into waking, there's a gentle tremor, a hand brushing against the side of a cradle, and the building creaks, a sound like a wooden ship complaining in a storm. My eyes flick to the glass of water on the bedside table. Vibrations ripple along its surface, but nothing more. Tatsu sleeps on.

Aki comes running into the room, his tiny steps like a tattoo on the shiny faux-wood of the corridor.

'Did you know cockroaches can live for a week without

their heads?' He scrambles onto the bed and hauls himself up to straddle my chest, so he can stare into my face for my reaction. He is panting slightly, despite the fact his bedroom is about five metres away.

'No, Aki-chan, I didn't know that. That's revolting. Where did you find that out?'

'Daisuke went to Ueno Zoo and saw a talk by the bug man. Can we go to Ueno Zoo? Why do you never take us anywhere?'

'We went to Ueno Zoo during the winter holidays, Aki. About three months ago. The week before we went to Tama Zoo. And you said you hated zoos, because the parrot sat on your head.'

'I don't remember,' Aki replies accusingly, as if I might be making it up or have somehow wiped his memory to spite him. He begins bouncing, apparently checking the flexibility of my rib cage.

'Aki, stop it, that hurts. *Aki.*'

He stops and swings his legs around so he has one heel on my trachea and the other on my upper lip.

'My feet are on your face,' he chortles appreciatively, his giggle still liquid, the laugh of a baby rather than a child. My eyes close again and I wonder if I can snatch ten more seconds of sleep in this position. The sole of his foot, brushing against my face, is flower-petal soft and I am suddenly so overcome by the babyness of him that I grab him and plant kisses all over his round cheeks and the top of his head, where it still smells exactly the way it did when he was newborn. As I roll over to tickle him, Aki asphyxiating with laughter, he throws out a foot which smacks Tatsu, a still sleeping mass, clean on the cheekbone. Tatsu roars and throws off the covers, standing up and managing to look magnificent in his indignation, despite wearing only his pants. Aki is awed and apologetic.

'Sorry Papa.'

Seeing Aki, Tatsu blinks sleep out of his eyes. He grunts, then throws himself back on the bed.

'I was *asleep*,' he tells Aki, poking him under the ribs, where Aki is the most ticklish. 'How *dare* you wake me up.' Aki is shrieking with glee, trying simultaneously to get away from Tatsu's tickling and put his arms around Tatsu's neck for a proper cuddle. Eventually Tatsu concedes and allows Aki to wrap himself round him, his face pressed up against his father's.

'You join the cuddle too, Mama,' Aki orders. 'I'm the ham in the sandwich.'

I put my arms around Aki, my face in his neck.

'What shall we do today?' I ask Tatsu conversationally. It's a Saturday, and the weather is warming up, hinting at spring. 'It's meant to be sunny – we could take a picnic to Shinjuku-Gyoen.'

Tatsu's eyes are closed again. 'You take them, Mizuki. I have to go into the office.'

'Papa, I want you to come.' Aki's voice is urgent. 'I need to show you my somersault I learnt in gymnastics at school.'

Tatsu smiles with his eyes closed. 'You show me after breakfast, Aki, and then Mama will take you to the park, okay?'

As the kids and I are leaving, I check the digital earthquake warning device by the door, as I always do, a tic that gets me nowhere. The earthquake mascot, Namazu, looks as much like a fat, whiskered raindrop as ever, totally chilled out about the havoc his namesake could wreak on us at any moment. Japanese legend says that earthquakes are caused by Namazu the giant catfish, who lives under the earth and is only kept from thrashing and wriggling by the god Kashima, who sits on his tail to keep him under control. Woe betide Kashima getting tired, or distracted, because that's when Namazu gets a big old tail flick in, trashing the ground above. A brilliant legend for a hard-working nation, really – take your eye off the ball at your own potentially fatal risk. No wonder we never relax.

That being the case, Aki, Eri and I still make a good go of it. The grass in Shinjuku-Gyoen is so lush and soft that when you take your shoes off, which we do as soon as we get there, it's like walking on a particularly luxurious shag pile rug. The children are so entranced by this that they invent an involved game about a magic carpet which entertains them almost all afternoon – which is a good thing because, despite it being a park, almost all other forms of entertainment are banned, as shown by large happy pictures with crosses through them at the entrance. No ball games, no musical instruments, no wheeled objects, no booze, of course. There are white-gloved guards at the entrance who have been known to open innocent-looking drinks and smell them, so seriously do they take their charge. Once you get past them, though, the restrictions guarantee such good behaviour and such pristine surroundings that rolling around on the grass in the sunshine has a certain sanitised Elysian quality, which can be appealing.

After we've counted the carp in all the ponds, and crossed and recrossed the numerous stone bridges under various fantasy guises, the five o'clock melody plays on the public tannoy, a segment from a traditional song about going home that never fails to make me feel nostalgic, despite hearing it every single day of my life. We get on our bicycles to head back, me buckling Aki into his seat on my handlebars as he carefully pulls all the stamen out of an azalea. Dusk is advancing as we cycle home, Eri following behind me like a duckling, and I can feel something familiar creeping underneath my rib cage, and then fading away. Restaurants and bars that have been closed during the day start to open, the illumination of their lights the start of the city's transformation. Wandering weekenders are beginning to make evening plans, pulling up a chair on a terrace for a drink, calling to friends.

As we make our way through Aoyama Cemetery, a huge expanse of greenery and history amid the modern thrum of the city, cawing crows rise up into a sky tinged pink and orange. The day has been warm, but with the setting sun the temperature drops, and as we cycle through an avenue of trees I can almost taste the dewy, plant-like cold on my skin. The street lamps haven't yet been lit and in the maze of Aoyama's backstreets, the light from grocers and fishmongers finishing up their day's trade is almost harsh in its brightness. The tantalising smells of food being prepared for evening service billow out of ventilators, and proprietors drag boards advertising happy hours and special menus onto pavements. In the twilight the city is expectant, waiting for the night, and its pulse makes mine beat faster, as it always does.

'Do you want to go out for tonkatsu, for supper?' I ask Eri on a whim. 'Papa won't be back till late tonight anyway.'

Her face lights up and she almost misses a revolution on her pedals.

'Yes, Mama!'

The feeling that's been lurking shows itself long enough for me to identify it, and then vanishes like a trail of smoke in a gust of wind. It's depression, or something like it. For a long time, the beautiful Tokyo sunset set me on a downward spiral, everything about it promising excitement, and intimacy and life, but not for me. I preferred to be firmly indoors while the sun worked its magic across the sky, cooking, bathing the children, so night could fall without me noticing and the evenings of clearing up by myself were just an extension of my days. Now, though, something's changed and the promise the sunset suggests doesn't seem to exclude me. Eri cycles up so she's alongside me and I find that I'm whistling. The sun starts to set and the air is electric with possibility, and now I can feel it too.

24

Between the invitation and the night of the dinner, I find out two things about Kiyoshi. First, he used to be married. To a Parisian. I am dying to quiz him on every aspect of this relationship; how it started, how it went, how it ended, what the wedding was like, what it's like to have sex in French, what they ate, where they lived, what language they spoke in, what they talked about. I spend hours imagining her sleeping face on the bed next to Kiyoshi – wavy blonde Rapunzel hair spread out across the pillow? Bright blue eyes when she opened them and smiled at him? She surely can't have looked like an actual Disney princess. Maybe she had a chic pixie cut and auburn hair, something that could be described as 'gamine'. Maybe she was too busy to smile at him and checked her watch and went '*Zut alors!*' and then rushed to pull on her effortlessly stylish workwear while he kissed her neck. I wonder if he sleeps naked.

Since I am only inwardly insane, I divulge none of this, obviously, but accept it coolly and offer my condolences about the divorce.

'It's better this way,' he says firmly.

'Do you still think about her?' Am I allowed to ask that?

There's an infinitesimal pause before he replies. 'Not any more.'

Second, Kiyoshi has not been living the life of a monk since the split. Attending the dinner will be some of his oldest friends, who lent him cash from credit cards when he opened his first izakaya and are now stakeholders in his restaurants. Their wives. And a woman who, it turns out, he had a short fling with and who he seems to wish wasn't coming.

'Why is she?' I ask a little too acidly. I imagine their relationship, cordial, loaded with nostalgia. I wonder how many short flings he's had, and something makes me feel like a cat that's been rubbed in the wrong direction. 'It's not a birthday party free-for-all. I thought it was a very important business meeting masquerading as a dinner.'

'But the masquerade has to be very, very good,' he explains. 'And I knew it would hurt her feelings if I didn't invite her.'

The dinner is one of those events where everyone is a little supercharged. Everyone's checking each other out, we all know we're on show, we're all looking our best and there's very expensive booze. Kami is just as beautiful inside as it promised to be the first time I saw it, with traditional private dining rooms leading off a raked gravel corridor lit with paper lanterns, and a rowdier central area with a circular bar constructed of saké bottles. The seating here is those tatami mats with a gully around the table, so you look like you're sitting on the floor but inflexible Westerners feel more comfortable. I'm wearing an asymmetric black dress I've been thinking about since Kiyoshi mentioned the evening, and that even made Tatsu look up momentarily as I left the apartment, to my consternation. Aki was already asleep; Eri at a fortuitous sleepover. Luckily it was only the sort of appraising look you might give to a particularly healthy-looking dog, or a very symmetrical tree, before he turned his eyes back to his screen.

The horrible fear of being overdressed vanishes the moment I see the rest of the group. Kiyoshi's friends are confident, at ease with each other in the way that only old friends can be, comfortable in their own skin. Their company fills me with a sense of anticipation, and a prickle of an unattractive, jealous longing that I brush away. I'm wondering who I'll be, what the first words out of my mouth will sound like. Whether today I'll be sweet and a little shy, or I'll just come out flat and awkward, or I'll end up making some filthy joke in the first thirty seconds.

'You must be Kiyoshi's friend Mizuki,' the beautiful woman opposite me says, touching my arm lightly with a perfectly manicured hand. 'It's so nice to meet you. I'm Tamao.'

And it turns out I can be myself – or at least the scrubbed-up version.

Kiyoshi is wearing a dark indigo shirt that somehow emphasises everything – the whiteness of his teeth, the line of his jaw, the muscles in his arms that I've always pretended not to notice. He's being proprietorial of everyone and very commanding of the staff. He smiles at me when I catch his eye for the first time, and when he comes around to pour me a drink, whispers, 'I'm glad you came.'

The people we're wooing are the Americans, a tall, languorous man who's cut his hair extremely short to hide the fact it has the consistency of candy floss, and a craggy one with an overly expressive face, whose wide, interested eyes and booming laugh threaten to turn against you at any moment.

As the evening goes on, I begin to work out the threads that connect people. The man over there, fantastically well-preserved and with the kindest face, must be married to the brash, glamorous lady who seems to be telling off Sotaro, the impossibly young and capable manager of Gion. Yoriko, Kiyoshi's PR, looks like she might not really be a drinker, bright red and giggling after her first glass, infinitely more approachable than in her haughty daytime guise. The foursome over there who clearly know each other a little better than the wider group, who laugh longer and harder the more they drink. Tamao, chatting demurely to the Americans in perfect English, who can be the only one Kiyoshi had a fling with. I'm talking to a bohemian architect seated next to me about his travels for work, which are genuinely interesting, but really I'm watching Tamao, seated opposite. She's very refined – everything about her is well-brought-up, well-educated, like a thoroughbred horse. If only she'd been wearing a mauve lace dress with a high collar that did nothing for her colouring – but she's wearing a silk printed shirt, linen culottes and expensive jewellery. She looks classy to the bone, and even though I forbid myself to, I wonder if I look like a bow-legged little girl from a field, playing dress-up in her fancy clothes. If that's his type, of course he'll never go for you, a treacherous voice in my head whispers, and I slam my focus back to the architect, who looks surprised. He's not meant to go for me. But my attention wanders back to her. My English is as good as yours. I wonder if you give good blowjobs or have a round bottom.

'So, Mizuki.' She turns her attention to me at that

inopportune moment. Please don't have noticed me staring. 'How do you know Kiyoshi?'

'He's a friend of my brother's,' I lie easily. 'I practically grew up with him.'

Kiyoshi has suddenly materialised next to me, pouring me another drink, and there's a thump in the middle of my rib cage, like a train speeding up and then braking too fast. He doesn't flinch.

'We used to do kendo together,' he concurs, looking straight at me. 'His kid sister was always hanging around. You got pretty good at kendo too, in the end, no?'

'Perhaps, eventually. Despite my clumsiness.' I have never had a kendo lesson in my life.

'Can I get you another drink, Tamao-san?'

The food, when it comes, is divine, and we all know the white dudes would be idiots not to let Kiyoshi open a new restaurant on the very spike of their building, in the position where the star would go on a Christmas tree. Just looking at the food is a feast – tessellations of the most lightly tempura'd maple leaves, arranged like a tree, a salad so green you want to peer at the colour of it, the delicately sliced okra punctuating the leaves like flowers in a meadow. And the flavour – tobiko explodes against the tongue like bubbles that taste of the ocean, a cold rush over just-warm rice, a morsel of tuna seared over something woody that tastes like a Nordic forest and swimming in the Pacific in one bite. We all close our eyes and melt into somebody else's memories.

'That's it for me, then,' Tamao declares after the first bite of the eel, meltingly soft and rich as caramel. 'This is the best unagi I've ever eaten. I'm never cooking again. There is no point in eating anything that isn't this food.'

'You can't not cook, Tama-chan,' Kiyoshi teases her. 'Your hayashi rice is the best.'

Tama-chan, says a sour little voice in my head, like a camp TV presenter who's swallowed a lemon. Like a Tamagotchi. Oh, Tama-chan.

As each dish arrives, conversation halts and all that can be heard is exclamations and semi-orgasmic murmurings. The only people who eat in silence are the foreigners, but I don't think it's the food – they never seem as vocal about it as we do. I'm sitting next to the craggy American, close enough to see how well-moisturised his skin is, and to notice that he picks the wakame seaweed out of his miso soup. When the rice arrives, each grain as fluffy and white as a cloud, he pours soy sauce carelessly over it, and even Tamao nearly chokes on her food before recovering herself and looking discreetly away. He's trying to tell some story about a Japanese director but has forgotten his name.

'You know, the guy who does all those martial arts movies,' he is saying impatiently. The only people nominally involved in the conversation apart from Kiyoshi and his entourage are Tamao and me, since we're the only ones who admit to speaking English. The man's accent drawls – I don't know where that means he's from, but it makes him harder to understand, and his mouth bigger. 'In the bamboo forests.'

'Oh, in Arashiyama? In Kyoto?' asks Tamao. 'I wonder who that could be?'

He is practically rolling his eyes at our ignorance. 'The ones where people fly.'

Surely not, but, '*Crouching Tiger, Hidden Dragon*?' I offer. 'Ang Lee? Zhang Yimou?'

'They're the most famous Japanese movies internation-ally!' the man chides, ignoring me completely. We all try to look chastened, apart from Kiyoshi, who is looking at me with open-faced amusement.

Having finished his meal, the man stabs his chopsticks vertically downwards into what is left of his rice, a rite that is only performed at funerals. The people around him just manage to resist a collective intake of breath and avert their eyes. Yoriko is staring at the chopsticks as if he has just flung a corpse on the table, and in her tipsy state is on the verge of saying something, when a waiter, alert to Kiyoshi's every eye movement, swoops in and removes the offending item. The group visibly exhales. I idly con-gratulate myself on the fact that Laurence would never do such a thing, being well-schooled in Japanese table man-ners. The American, oblivious, reaches for his glass and has it halfway to his lips when the answer comes to him in a flash of inspiration. 'Zhang Zhimou! How can none of you know Zhang Zhimou!' He shakes his head. 'That lion movie with ninjas in it, best film ever made.' He points his glass at Tamao. 'Zhang Zhimou – don't forget the name. Next time there's a movie of his out, you get yourself to that movie theatre.' He takes a sip of his drink. 'Make you see your country in a whole new light, I guarantee you.'

Kiyoshi's shoulders are shaking and he appears to have tears in his eyes. He gets up, ostensibly to go and supervise some activity behind the scenes. Not one of us is impolite enough to point out that the country in question isn't ours.

Later, when the incident has become merely one of many, but we're all too full of good food and good booze to care, the conversation at our end turns inevitably towards business, and Tamao and I distance ourselves politely, by the simple expedient of speaking Japanese to each other.

'Where did you learn to speak such good English?' I ask her.

'We learnt at school,' she says using the formal phrasing, smiling. 'Then I continued at university and I went to London briefly, to work and study further.'

'And what do you do for work?'

'Well, I studied law to please my father,' she says with an adorable laugh. 'But I'm not sure it's for me. I'm working at an American firm at the moment.'

'That must be so interesting. You must work very hard.'

'No harder than anyone else,' she says, still smiling, modest, the model woman. No harder than almost physically impossible, then. 'I hear you have children, Mizuki.'

It's almost a surprise to remember that I do. 'Yes, two children.'

'How wonderful. It must be wonderful to have a family.'

She's right, of course, even though I don't know what to say. 'I'm very lucky,' I manage. There is a little pause where we both smile and think about the other's wonderful life.

'Is a family on your agenda?' I ask, to fill the gap, and then hope it wasn't a completely inappropriate thing to say.

'I've always felt that being a mother would be a full-time job in itself,' Tamao says carefully. 'It would be very difficult to commit yourself to two jobs. There's a lot of travelling involved in my line of work. I think that, to do it properly, women can probably only do one or the other, don't you?'

'Maybe,' I say guardedly. 'Although they seem to manage it in the West.'

'That's true,' says Tamao smoothly. 'They do lots of things differently in the West.' Which is almost always code for 'and not as well as we do'. It's one of those conversations where all I'm finding out about Tamao is that she knows how to play an upright, hardworking Tokyoite with conventional opinions. Either that, or she is one.

Eventually, we're the last table in the restaurant and people start to leave.

'It was so nice to meet you, Mizuki,' Tamao tells me, and I notice how pretty her eyes are. Well-educated, successful, stylish – it's a shame I can't hate her. Kiyoshi approaches as she's putting on her coat, collarless and corn-flower blue, European-looking.

'So, I'll see you in New York then,' she says to him, in a way that suggests they've discussed it previously. Maybe I can hate her. They move towards the door, locked in that smiling, last-chance, parting conversation, and I make moves to find my coat.

'Mizuki, wait,' Kiyoshi calls, and I kick myself for the joy that rushes through me. 'I'll call you a taxi.'

I start to remind him we're in Tokyo, where the only way to hail a taxi is to stand out in the street, but the swarthy American is muttering something serious at him, so I nod. The other guests trickle out and I stand with my hands in my coat pockets, not sure where to look. The ikebana on the table in front of me is a work of art, an explosion of violets against shy sweet stems of pussy willow. How did he work it all out, all the endless details that make it perfect? The gulf between us suddenly seems laughable – he who built this, and will go so far, and me wondering if I'll get around to ordering a missing puzzle piece. I imagine his restaurant at the top of the world.

I wonder if Cassie will read about it in wherever cool new places get written up, and book a table for a birthday dinner, or an anniversary, and take photographs of beautiful people smiling widely. And then Kiyoshi will invite Tamao there one night, when she's in town for business, and she'll walk in in her power heels and designer suit and he'll realise what erudite, high-class goods he's been missing, and they'll have sex on the bar top, looking down on New York. She'll be slightly reluctant at first, being so refined, but eventually her ardour for him and the hotness of the surroundings will win her over, and it'll be the best night of their lives.

For god's sake.

Kiyoshi and the Americans are finishing up. There are firm handshakes and pats on the back, and last thank yous and promises, eyes crinkled up with sincerity. The Americans depart. Kiyoshi waits for the door to close behind them, and five seconds more. Then he gives a little whoop, and all the staff, who have secretly been watching the proceedings from their various posts, start to cheer and clap.

'Everyone have a drink,' Kiyoshi calls. 'Great job, guys.' He grins at me, standing there in my coat like a lemon. 'Stay for one more?' He's euphoric.

'I can't,' I hear myself saying apologetically. 'You should celebrate with your guys. It was an amazing night.' And I mean it, truly, so happy for him, and ashamed that my sudden flatness is in direct correlation with his high.

'Really?'

'Yeah, I have to get up with the kids in the morning.' Because that's the world I live in, I want to remind him,

145

like a spoilt child stamping on someone's foot to get their attention. Walk on by, my friend.

'Okay.'

I start to say good night, and thank you, but he indicates that he'll walk me out, shaking the hands of his waiting staff as he goes. Out of the main room and down the entrance hall, we are alone, the paper screens to the private dining rooms closed, the golden light from the lanterns dancing on the wood and gravel. Neither of us speaks. For some reason, my chest is constricting.

'Thanks so much for inviting me,' I say. 'You did an incredible job. Your restaurant is beautiful. They'd be stupid not to want you in New York.' I smile, avoiding his eye, and go to open the door. The air outside is cold.

'Mizuki,' he says, putting his hand on the door. On my hand, as it happens. 'Why did you tell Tamao I was a friend of your brother's?'

Embarrassment, and indignation that he should embarrass me, makes me look straight at him. I thought he'd be laughing at me, but his face is searching, his eyes on mine. Because I couldn't explain how we met. Because I couldn't say what I thought this was. Because I didn't want her to know me, and I wanted to save a little piece of you for myself.

'I'm a compulsive liar,' I throw at him. 'And so are you, it turns out.'

He half smiles, as if I've disappointed him in some way, and lets go of the door, and his taking his hand off mine is such a loss that I walk out quickly, without looking back. I can't see him again, is what I'm thinking as I stalk down the path away from him. Everything's fine, I haven't made a total fool of myself, it's salvageable if I just don't see him again.

I don't hear the door open, don't hear his steps behind me.

'Mizuki,' and the way he says it, my skin stands up and it's as if nobody has ever said my name before.

I turn around. He lifts his hand and runs the back of his index finger down the side of my face, and I don't move because all I am is my racing heart. He's looking at me, and it's the wrong moment because my eyes are giving too much away. His are saying something too, but I don't believe it, I don't dare to believe it, until he kisses me.

25

Spring erupts the very next day. It's Saturday, and when we leave in the morning, me to take Eri to a swimming lesson and Tatsu to practise baseball with Aki in the park, the trees lining the avenue in front of our building are fresh and green. By the time we return for lunch, the cherry blossom has bloomed and the avenue is a hyperbolic froth of pink cloud, the entire area transformed.

'We could practically have sat and watched it happen,' Tatsu says, looking up at the thousand tiny faces of just-born flowers. The blossom, a surprise celebration bestowed on everybody, makes staying indoors impossible, the mood of the entire city too buoyant to sit still. We get on our bikes, Aki perched in his seat at the front of mine, and follow the blossom until we find an area where traders have set up makeshift stalls with tables under the trees.

'I'll be out for the office hanami on Monday, now,' Tatsu remarks through his grilled onigiri. 'They'll get a couple of the guys to stay over in Ueno Park Sunday night, I guess, to save a space. I wonder who it'll be this year.'

I try, and fail, to summon up a relevant name from

among Tatsuya's colleagues. 'Who's newest? They'll send them, right?'

Tatsu nods. 'Maybe Masakun,' he muses. 'He's only been with the company four months.'

'Don't you kind of wish you could sleep under the blossom in the park on Sunday night?' I ask. 'It's warm enough. I bet it's beautiful.' In my current mood, the idea is bliss. But then, pretty much everything is bliss.

We stay out all afternoon, cycling from one park to another, even as it grows dark. For weeks before, workmen have been busy attaching uplighters to the cherry blossom trees, waiting for them to bloom so they could be lit from below in all their glory. In the balmy evening, people park themselves everywhere with picnic suppers and beers from the convenience store, on benches, perched on walls, even with little mats that they take their shoes off to sit on, slap bang in the middle of the pavement. The atmosphere in Tokyo is always cordial, considerate, and now it's as if we're all guests at a spectacular wedding who don't know each other – a feeling of excitement and goodwill binds us all. Food stalls have popped up all over the city, and shops are crammed with promotional cherry blossom products – flavoured sweets in the combini, limited edition sakura coffee cups in the cafés. We sit for a while in a beer garden, the children playing around us, time running on and everyone too full of the joys of spring to care. Aki and Eri scoop up the soft petals that have already started to fall, and delight in throwing them in the air, making snowstorms and confetti. I have a vague feeling that a reckoning is around the corner, but for now, everything is perfect. I wish I could exist in suspended animation, every aspect of this moment as it is.

Tatsu's phone rings. He jumps up as if he's just been shot.

'Yes,' he barks into the phone, his demeanour altered in an instant. Aki comes running over to show him something, and Tatsu wards him off with an imperious finger. As Tatsu strides away, frowning, Aki's face looks on the verge of crumbling.

'Aki-chan,' I call urgently. 'Aki, will you show me? What is it?'

'I wanted to show Papa!' His voice is wavering, unsure whether to sob or throw a fit. To stop him chasing Tatsu, I plant him on my lap.

'Is it a petal? Hey, Aki, have you ever tried whistling with it?'

'I wanted to show Papa!' His voice is rising.

'I used to be able to do this when I was a little girl,' I tell him, trying to ignore the fact he is flailing to get away from me and after his father. 'Want to see?' I manage to manoeuvre both hands around him to pull the tiny petal tight and blow, and the petal emits a high-pitched, trombone-ish blast. Aki is instantly still, his face transformed.

'Mama, it's a singing fart!' he shouts, exploding into laughter. 'Do it again! I'll go get you some more petals.' He runs away in the direction of his sister. 'Eri, see what Mama can do!'

By the time Tatsu comes back to tell us curtly he is going into work, Eri and Aki are in fits of giggles from the variety of scatological sounds they've coaxed the petals into producing.

'What time will you be back?' I ask him.

'I have no idea, Mizuki.'

'I was just asking. You don't need to bark at me.'

'Well, how do I know what time I'm going to be back? It might not take that long but it might take until five in the morning. I have no idea.'

The truth, the absolute truth, is that I'm glad he used that tone of voice. When we get home, Aki and Eri too wired to sleep, the three of us watch *Totoro* again, Aki still a little afraid of the storm at the beginning, still shouting at Mei, as she gets lost, to turn back, to take the other road. As I tuck them into bed later that night, I find that I'm humming to myself.

There's no word from Kiyoshi that day, which is of no consequence. Or all of the next day, and everything is fine because I'm not a fifteen-year-old and I don't check my phone every thirty seconds or suffer from arrhythmia just because a strange man has kissed me. I would be hard pushed, though, to explain why, on receiving a message in the evening from a number saved under 'Ichiko' that asks if I want to go to Nakameguro to see the blossom on Monday, I have to go into the bathroom to do a little victory dance, and then peer at my reflection in the mirror because I look so damn happy.

26

Nakameguro is rammed with people; tentative first dates, elderly couples, groups of selfie-taking teenagers, tourists. I've disembarked from the train having convinced myself that Kiyoshi has invited me out specifically to tell me that he finds me physically repulsive, and am disproportionately relieved to see him looking relaxed, ribbing me as usual. We start along the canal bank in the crowd, walking at a snail's pace, hemmed in on all sides by jubilant holidaymakers. The sun glints off the water, and above us, the blossom is serene in its magnificence.

'Every year, I forget just how phenomenal it is,' Kiyoshi says. 'I always think it can't come as quickly as I imagined, and it can't be as dense as I made up in my head.'

As well as the flowers on the trees, the telegraph poles have been dolled up for the occasion, decorated with branches of fake blossom, interspersed with flags and hanging decorations.

'It is amazing,' I agree. And then because there is a millisecond pause and I'm nervous, 'But I also think it looks kind of frog-spawny.'

'What?'

'You know, like frog spawn. There's so much of it, all that bubbly white with the little black dots in the middle.' Kiyoshi is smiling at me, a broad smile, intoxicating. 'Like the stuff we used to have in the school pond,' I continue uncontrollably. 'Before they turned into tadpoles and we took them into the classroom in jam jars. Like ponds of spunk.'

He breaks into a guffaw, the guffaw that is so lovely to me, I almost find myself thinking, and says, 'Well cheers, Mizuki, I think you've ruined hanami for me forever.'

'I'm not saying it's not absolutely gorgeous,' I object.

'Just gorgeous like frog spawn.'

We shuffle along in the crowd, the salty-sweet aromas of the yakitori and kasutera cooking in the roadside stalls tantalising. There are people sitting in the open balconies of the riverside cafés, stretched out in seating, smugly looking down at us groundlings, kings of all they survey.

'I used to live in an apartment there,' Kiyoshi tells me, indicating with his chin at a small, insalubrious block with minute windows facing the river. 'We used to rent out the fire escape during hanami for so much money it covered our rent for three months. And charge people to use the toilet, too.'

'A businessman to the core.'

'That's me.'

And your Parisian wife, I want to ask, did she live there with you? Were you ecstatically happy in your artist's garret? Did you sometimes climb onto the fire escape at 3 a.m., after hours spent fucking, to gaze together at the midnight blossom, ghostly in the dark, reflected on the water? Worse, did you do that with Tamao? The thoughts make me feel quiet.

We walk on for a few minutes, the silence between us comfortable. When I first feel the side of his hand against mine, I assume it's accidental.

'Those guys from New York,' Kiyoshi says conversationally. 'They liked Kami.'

Our hands are still touching.

'Well obviously. The guy didn't know one Asian country from another but even he would know how great Kami is.'

'They think it's going to go ahead. It's not a hundred per cent confirmed, but they said they're pretty sure they want to give me something on the top floor.'

'Kiyoshi,' and even though nobody could have doubted the outcome, I'm elated for him. 'That's incredible,' and because the words are weak, and I can't throw my arms around him, I end up gripping my fist at him like a bad softball coach. Kill me now.

'Stop, you're making me blush.' He bats away my terrible fist and turns his face away in a parody of embarrassment, bringing my hand down without letting go of it. In the two seconds that I don't flinch, don't move my hand away, he links his fingers with mine. All of me, every particle, is focused on our interlinked fingers, the feel of his skin, warm and dry, on mine.

'You big geek,' I say, looking straight ahead. The crowd is so dense, nobody can see. 'Did you ever see the Twin Towers when they were there?' I ask him, for something to say, something to tide the moment over, so the shock of the novelty won't make him let go.

'Once. A friend I made in France ended up working there, and I met him for lunch when I was in New York.'

'What were you doing in New York?'

'Honeymoon.' But even that doesn't matter with my hand in his. 'Well, part of it.'

'What happened to your friend?' It's only when the words are out of my mouth that I think it might be a bad question.

'He got out. He was one of those very decisive guys, didn't take any crap from anybody.'

'Very French?' I offer.

'Yes,' Kiyoshi smiles, remembering. 'He was in the second tower, and when the first tower was hit, he got the elevator down.'

'Shit.'

'Yeah. He said he only just made it.' He shakes his head. 'If he'd just waited a few seconds, not been sure what to do . . .'

I shudder. 'That would be me,' I lament. 'I'd be worrying that I'd look like a dick if I ran away too fast, so I'd stay and die instead.'

He gives me an incredulous look, our linked hands now a matter of fact. 'Well, maybe fix that,' he suggests. 'Don't die rather than look like a dick.'

'That's reasonable advice,' I agree, and he squeezes my hand. 'What about you?' But I know the answer.

'I'd get out, clearly,' he states with confidence. 'Whose definition of "dick" is it anyway? You want to get some food?'

We inch our way out of the crowd, and as our cover thins, we automatically release our hands. We find a small restaurant down a side street and sit outside sharing plates of steaming gyōza and drinking beer. Our conversation

155

is the same as it has always been, comfortable, sarcastic, flowing, and I'm almost disappointed that something hasn't changed.

'Do I have anything in my teeth?' I demand at the end of the meal, baring them unattractively.

Kiyoshi laughs. 'No.'

'Good.'

He looks down at the bill, reaching for his wallet as I reach for mine. 'And even if you did, you'd still be perfect,' he says. 'Huh, I'm a bit short on cash. Can you lend me 500 yen?'

I definitely misheard him. 'I'm feeling so generous today,' I tell him, 'I'll *give* you 500 yen.'

We stand up and he stretches, satisfied, and the taut skin of his torso shows above his jeans. I so badly want to grab hold of him that I run down the street as fast as I can with my arms out, then back to the other end. The frenetic, upbeat rhythms of a song from some unknown TV manga have started in my head and I feel like I'm on drugs.

'What are you doing?' Kiyoshi demands, laughing, grabbing hold of me as I fly by.

Public displays of affection are not a thing in Tokyo. But the smell of his skin, the feel of his hair under my fingers and I don't care about anything else on earth. He steps closer so our bodies are pressed against each other and I know that I'll never be able to get as much of him as I want. Let's go somewhere, anywhere, I don't care where, let's go – but I don't know if I said it, or he did, or if there were no words. Eventually I hear him, like someone half-awake, his breath hot in my ear, 'I want to see you again.'

'Well, obviously,' I mutter, flippant to the last.

'Tonight, I want to see you tonight,' and I don't even need to hear the urgency in his voice to say, 'Yes,' without another thought. Yes, yes, yes.

So presumably the time for reconsidering would have been that afternoon, as I collected the children from their activities and texted Elena, Eloise's adorable Filipina nanny, to ask her to babysit that evening. It could have gone sordid and stale, the organisation of it, the waiting, but I was too high for my feet to touch the ground. I'm good at compartmentalising too, so I was an especially devoted mother that afternoon, without complicated feelings, just something that spilled out once in a while, so I spun Aki round and round by his hands, to his delight. Elena arrived once the children were in bed, and I nearly hugged her.

The total lack of spontaneity in meeting that evening should have been enough to put me off completely, or start to go for it and realise five minutes in that the situation made me so awkward I'd rather peel my skin off than go through with it. Maybe if Kiyoshi hadn't been looking the other way when I saw him first, that night, so it was like I could discover him all over again. Maybe if he'd told me where we were going, instead of just leading me there, and if he hadn't kissed me in the elevator going up. Maybe.

The spring passed in a blur, punctuated by things I'll never forget. Aki's first day at proper school, with his grey shorts and black randoseru, Tatsu crouching down to look into his face for some man-to-man advice before he left in the morning, Aki's chubby knees still so baby-like I didn't want to let him go. Then came the monsoon, warm and relentlessly wet, the perfect time to spend afternoons holed up indoors, one way or another. The smell of the hollow at the base of Kiyoshi's neck. His eyes on mine. The imprint of my nails on his shoulders like puncture marks. The scattering of tiny moles on his torso, like a constellation.

27

'You can't look at my tanzaku, Mama,' Aki tells me importantly from behind the enormous bough of bamboo he is brandishing, its branches festooned with colourful origami decorations. The rainy season is over and summer has undeniably arrived, so that Aki is permanently pink-cheeked and tousle-haired. In his haste to rush out of the school door, he's dislodged his hat and it sits crooked on his head. He pauses for half a second. 'Actually, you can.'

His classroom is disgorging children armed with bamboo, enthusiastically attacking their uncertain-looking mothers.

He hurries towards me, jabbing me with the stick. 'Look, see this one?' He shoves the branch into my hands as he combs through its foliage for one of his paper messages. 'Read it.'

'"I wish for a hamster,"' I read, his letters enormous and so carefully formed. He's barely been at school three months. 'You're such a clever boy, Aki! Look at your beautiful writing!'

He grins, his chest puffed out with pride. 'And this one, Mama.'

'"I wish to go to the seaside."' I feel inordinately pleased that the tanzaku wishes are containable, grantable. Some paper evidence to grab hold of that, despite my parenting flaws, the children are happy. 'We're going Aki, in the summer holidays. We'll go stay with Obāchan after Obon, remember? And we can go to the beach every day.'

'Is Papa coming?'

'Maybe. We'll see.' Maybe for two days, possibly three. Possibly.

'We learnt the story in school,' he says, as we make our way out of the gate hand in hand, me holding the bamboo aloft like a staff.

'Did you, Aki-chan? How does it go?'

'Well,' he looks very serious, and looks up at me to ensure I'm giving him my full attention. 'Orihimé was the princess who did beautiful weaving. Her daddy was the king of *everything*. Then one day Orihimé met Hikoboshi, who herds the sheep, and they loved each other so they played and played all day long.'

'That sounds fun.'

'Yes, but her daddy was cross that they both didn't do their work any more, so he put them on opposite sides of the big river and told them they could never meet again.'

The stars Vega and Altair, on opposite sides of the Milky Way. The ultimate Japanese love story.

'Never?'

Aki growls at me for interrupting. 'I'm about to *say* that. Orihimé cried and cried and was so sad that in the end her daddy said they could meet once a year, on Tanabata! That's next week. That's why we decorate the bamboo because on Tanabata Orihimé and Hikoboshi can play together again. And maybe they're so happy they'll make our wishes come true?' he suggests. 'But only if it's sunny.'

'Only if it's sunny?' This part of the story I hadn't remembered.

'Yes,' says Aki, like *duh*, 'because otherwise the birds can't go over the river to make the bridge, so then Orihimé and Hikoboshi can't cross over. And then they won't be able to play till next year.' Aki looks thoughtful. 'Mama, when we get home shall we make a teru-teru bōzu so it doesn't rain?' I, too, would trust the power of a paper dolly hanging in the window, made by Aki, over meteorological probability.

'That's a perfect idea, Aki. Let's do that. And shall we take your bamboo to the river at the weekend, to float it away, like we did with Eri's last year?'

'Yes!' He strokes his bamboo stick lovingly. 'And then maybe I'll get a hamster.' He's silent for a moment. 'Mama, poor Orihimé and Hikoboshi. They really wanted to play together.'

'I know. Do you think they should have been allowed to?'

'Yes.' My son is un-Japanese, still, choosing pleasure over duty. 'People could have used other things for making dresses, like leaves. Orihimé didn't really need to weave it. And the sheeps would have liked it better if Hikoboshi let them run around by themselves anyway.' Aki sighs, a deep sigh. 'Everybody is always getting in the way of playing.'

He's so serious a laugh bursts from my throat. 'Aki-chan, don't you have enough time to play?'

'No. Mama, can you make okonomiyaki for supper? On the hot plate on the table?'

'Isn't it a bit hot for okonomiyaki?' The light, tinkling

sound of a bell catches our attention and we look up to see a little black-and-white cat running past a wind chime, a row of delicate glass half-spheres painted with fireworks and goldfish. The cat gives us an innocent, wide-eyed look before disappearing around the corner, leaving the coloured bell pulls fluttering in the breeze.

'I'm going to write a new tanzaku asking for a cat. No, Mama, okonomiyaki is really good for today,' Aki says.

28

The children are in bed, and I'm washing up the dishes, playing over Kiyoshi's anatomy in my mind. The back of his ear as it curves into his neck, down to the place above his collarbone where I can see his pulse, the power in his arms, his perfect hands.

'Mizuki,' Tatsu calls from the living room.

'I'm finishing the washing-up.' After all the years I've spent with him not seeing me, I don't see him any more either. We exist like two blind fish, sliding past each other cordially in our parallel universes. It's a great solution.

'Mizuki, can you come here for a second?'

I step out from the kitchen, still wearing the rubber gloves. I'd expected him to be looking at a screen of some kind while he called me, scrolling through his phone or watching the soccer when he thought of something. It is disconcerting to find that he is looking at me. For a second, I feel as if my secrets are written all over me, then I rally and survey him coolly. I've been in something like a drunk haze, and Tatsu looking at me feels like the threat of sobering up.

'What is it?'

'Do you want to watch a film?'

It's a shame that my immediate reaction to this tentative offering is instinctive.

'No, I'm busy.'

'Okay. No worries.' He looks slightly crestfallen.

I go back into the kitchen and scrub the mābō-dōfu pan with vigour. I've never quite got used to the feeling of washing up with gloves on; there's something perverse about the sensation of warm water through a rubber barrier. Finished, I place them carefully on the side of the sink and go back into the sitting room.

'What are you going to watch?' This time, he'll rebuff me and that'll be that.

'Not sure.' He looks at me again. Like I'm someone he's speaking to. Like we are having a normal conversation. 'Maybe the new James Bond? We never got to go see it.' Because he was working late every night of its cinema release. Last year that comment would have made me prickle like a hedgehog and remind him of all the times he stood me up. This year I went to an afternoon showing with Kiyoshi, and all I feel is sorry for him that he missed it altogether. I like Tatsu so much more now that I need him less. He used to love films, foreign ones, old ones, new ones, every genre, watching directors compulsively, noticing the quirks that appeared in film after film, the actors they used repeatedly in bit-parts, the way their style developed over the years. When we were first dating, I'd use my English to impress him, telling him when the subtitles were off-key, introducing him to the films Cassie and I had watched as teenagers, thanking my lucky stars that Cassie had been weirdly discerning. I used to love watching them with him, his anticipation as they began, his total absorption, his determination that I share his enthusiasm. Now that I think about it, it's been years since we watched a movie together. I sit down next to him on the sofa.

'Sure, if you want. Or another Kurosawa?' Tatsu was obsessed, and in the early days we went to countless arthouse cinemas to see rereleases of *Yojimbo* and *Rashomon*. I'm not that keen; the insane villains and shrieking women don't do it for me, but he doesn't know that.

He lights up, turning so his whole body is facing me. 'Yeah? You want to?'

'Sure.'

He finds a film and I make some tea and dig out the osenbei I know he likes, and we sit together on the sofa like an elderly couple, chortling at the same things.

'That woman – isn't she the one—'

'—who was in that shit movie about the monk in the mountain.'

'That actress has a mouth like Eri.'

'You can't say that, she's evil!'

When the film is finished, he takes our cups to the kitchen and washes them up, and I turn out the lights in the sitting room, and we go to brush our teeth together, discussing the film through toothpaste foam. In bed, he rolls over with his back to me, like always, then turns to look at me and smile shyly. He looks like Aki.

'Thanks for letting me watch that film. I know you didn't like it.'

'I did!'

'Mizu, you've never liked Kurosawa's films. You're sweet.'

He rolls over again, still smiling. It's the most disturbed I've felt in months.

29

Maybe the only difference between Tatsu and Kiyoshi is the difference between reality and illusion, or how far they're willing to conspire with me on it. I had a boyfriend once who thought the way towards intimacy and closeness was to peel away the surrounding layers of crap until you could bare your soul. Even the phrase 'bare your soul' makes me feel sick and think of those weird breast-shaped custard puddings they sometimes sell in station souvenir shops. His method of achieving this dubious epiphany was to constantly pick apart everything I said. 'You don't mean that.' 'I wonder why you feel that way.' 'You're just saying that because you've been conditioned to. What do you really think?'

Unsurprisingly, it didn't last very long – apart from the fact he had good teeth and hair (as if I were choosing a racehorse), I have no idea what attracted me to him in the first place. I suppose the burning ardour of his attention was flattering – until it was toxic, with its constant implication that I didn't understand myself, that he knew me better than I did, that I needed to bring an end to all my pretence and walk around with only my paltry true self on show. Like a bald bird, maybe a turkey, with its neck hangings that remind me of scrotums, or a pasty nudist. That faux-analysis is something Tatsuya never did; either because he didn't mind that I was full of crap, or because he bought it. Maybe in all those years of happy marriage, Tatsu thought that Nice Wife Mizuki was the Real Me and was disappointed when the fault lines started to appear.

Nice Wife Mizuki is a version of the real me, for sure, and in all those years, I thought there was a strong possibility she could become the main model. Why not? What are we, apart from the stories we tell ourselves and other people? I know all too well that I'm a flimsy construct, a flamboyant playset shot through with exaggerations and inconsistencies and secret compartments full of unsavoury surprises. I made myself that way. Kiyoshi knew it all from the start and never needed to call me on it; he caught my bullshit and rumbled out a laugh, applauded my smoke and mirrors like the artwork it is. And I knew he did it too, a god of a man pockmarked with flaws that he hides in his shadows so all you see is his light. Maybe that's why it sometimes felt like we were perfect for each other.

30

The morning after we watch the film, I'm clearing away the breakfast dishes when I realise Tatsu has left his phone on the table. Unusually, he broke his stride from the bedroom to the door to steal a bite of Eri's toast before they walked to the station together, him to take one Metro line to work, and her another to school. Aki is feigning illness, having greeted me this morning with one eye shut and an expression like a snarling pirate, clutching his stomach and groaning. We both know it's bollocks, but for some reason the sight of Tatsu and Eri departing together made me let him off, and now he's building a town out of wooden blocks under the table, all stomach complaints forgotten, pleased as punch, and it feels deliciously like we're both playing truant.

'Papa's forgotten his phone,' I tell him, and even as I do, it begins to vibrate with messages. I watch their opening lines scroll across the screen with interest, almost willing there to be something scandalous.

Aki is making theatrical yelping sounds under the table. I stick my head under to see what he's doing. 'Aki? We're going to have to go to Papa's office to take it to him.'

'The mayor of the town is eating everybody, Mama! The rabbits don't like it!'

'No, I bet they don't.'

'What happens when you go into someone's tummy?'

Since we're only going on a short, singular mission, I'm almost discombobulated by how quickly Aki and I manage to leave the apartment, carrying next to nothing. I'd failed to take into account that we were travelling at rush hour, which Tatsu leaves early to avoid. I hold tightly onto Aki's hand, the speed of our walking dictated by the river of people carrying us down the stairs to the platform. We position ourselves neatly in the queue for the door, indicated by the lines painted on the platform floor, and when the train arrives, though not one person disembarks, we are impelled hopelessly into it by the polite, insistent force of the crowd behind us, and the white-gloved guard standing by the door, bowing efficiently before pushing any overhanging limbs neatly in, sealing the doors shut as if we're unruly underpants in a suitcase. Once we're inside, my shoulders practically dislocating thanks to the small space I'm trying to fit myself into, I peer down at my legs. I can feel Aki's arms around them, but not see his face.

'Aki-chan?' I wonder if he's going to suffocate.

He wriggles his head round and grins up at me, unbothered by the squash.

At Roppongi station, the escalator glides us up through the enormous atrium, bedecked with floating balloon Doraemons, the cat-robot from the future, for the release of the new movie in the summer holidays. At the top looms Roppongi Hills Mori building, a fifty-four-floor complex of business, commerce and residences conquering the sky, the only space in Tokyo left to expand into. The army of suits around us move as one, swarming their hive at a civilised but insistent pace, the matching shiny blackness of hundreds of heads giving the appearance of a sea of helmets, the greys and muted blues of the suits and jackets a uniform.

Aki trips and I catch him from falling, a disruption in the perfect regularity of movement.

'Your shoelace, Aki,' I say and lead him to a bench on one side of the entrance, causing a ripple of surprise that someone has changed direction.

When we stand up again a few moments later, the rhythm of the thinning crowd has changed like the speed being turned up on a travelator, the hive mind reprogrammed by some directive Aki and I can't see. With no change of expression, no heavy breathing and no self-consciousness, the men and women in suits are now running from the escalator towards the glass doors leading into the Mori building.

'Why are they running, Mama?' Aki asks. It's not a jog for show, a few steps of half-hearted speeding up to get to a door someone is holding open, it's a focused sprint with everyone participating, a race of evenly matched mono-chromatic contestants in corporate apparel and, in the case of the women, high heels. The clock by the entrance shows 08.56.

'I think they don't want to be late,' I tell him and, as I do, I remember being at school, sweeping the classroom after hours with the other students on the cleaning rota, and seeing the latecomers at baseball practice, even those who'd missed the mark by under a minute, being made to run around the pitch for the entirety of the session.

It never happened to me, because girls didn't attend, and I wasn't enough of a mug to make the tennis or netball squad, where we would have to practise for two hours before school every single day. I only started doing sports in New York with Cassie, where we were high-fived and affirmed for bothering to turn up to practice at all. Better dead than late, we say here.

The people running past us are avoiding looking at each other, but when they do catch someone's eye, they bow their heads in an apologetic movement, an acknowledgement of the shame collectively felt at the possibility of letting the side down.

'We're sometimes late for school,' Aki comments helpfully.

Inside the building, there is silence apart from the thrum of decisive heels tapping quickly on marble. I put my hands on Aki's shoulders to hold him out of the way, and we watch the mesmeric ballet of arriving runners clicking through the turnstiles and slotting into the lifts like pieces in a puzzle, straightening hair and patting down clothes, so that by the time the lift doors close, all are facing forwards with their hands folded in front of them, present, correct, immaculately attired.

At 08.59, Aki and I cautiously make our way through the turnstiles and board a completely empty elevator. Aki starts to sing to himself, a catchy classic about his favourite meal, omurice, but the song fades abruptly as the elevator doors open onto the reception area of Tatsu's office, a study in glass and marble with so much echoing space that every word I speak in the short exchange with the receptionists seems magnified and performative. Silently, Aki slips his hand into mine, smiles tightly at the polite greeting of one of the younger receptionists, and doesn't remove it even when we're shown to Tatsu's office, where Tatsu is on another phone, standing at the floor-to-ceiling window, surveying the city below him. For a moment, seeing him in this foreign land, facing away from us, he's somebody I don't know, and I am too. A handsome businessman, and his demure, helpful wife, and the picture fills me with nostalgia for a couple we have never been. He glances round when he sees us, surprised, and smiles a thank you when I hold up his phone, but is distracted by something the person on the other end has said. I can feel Aki tugging gently at my hand to leave. His father is a stranger here, a king or a prisoner, and either way nothing to do with the affectionate playmate he can be at home. I feel something like regret for having brought Aki here, as if I've shown him something I should have protected him from for a little longer, even if it is only an office building. His turquoise Shinkansen t-shirt pops against the colours of the office, and the thought of something so small and bright believing that being a cog in this tightly programmed machine is the only option for the future makes Tatsu's enormous office claustrophobic. Don't worry, I want to tell him, you can be a mountaineer, or a graffiti artist, or a lion-tamer. Why do all the other options that spring to mind sound so unlikely, and vaguely threatening?

I put Tatsu's phone down on his desk. Tatsu's eyes watch us leave, but he is engrossed in his conversation. The open-plan section Aki and I walk through back to the reception and the lift is permeated by concentrated quiet, the superior silence of libraries. I have a terrible urge to start singing Aki's omurice song at the top of my voice.

We don't go straight home, but stop for a while in

the huge open terrace at the bottom of the building, underneath the egg sac of the avant-garde spider statue, spiking above everything like something out of a nightmare, impressive and suffocating all at once. Here, wide arches and walkways lead into a gleaming complex of designer shops, modern art suspended from ceilings and the calming glimmer of water features. I sit on a bench and notice the rectangular manholes and slots in the ground behind it; Kiyoshi told me that most parks are fitted with underground equipment that can transform into toilets with cubicles and wash basins, turning open public areas into functioning evacuation spaces when the long-awaited earthquake of earthquakes finally arrives, and now I see them everywhere. The Mori building rises above us like a monolith, its smooth, shiny sides deflecting everything, giving nothing away, my view of it sliced in half by one of the gargantuan spider legs. A shrine to order, conformity, productivity, functionality. For a moment I feel as if I've stepped outside of myself, that it's impossible that this landscape could support human beings at all.

'Mama,' Aki says from where he is busy running his fingers through an artificial waterfall. 'When I grow up, I'm going to be a fireman. Or maybe a Power Ranger.'

3 1

When I finally spot Kiyoshi on the grass in Yoyogi Park, I jump off my bicycle and run towards him. He's thrown onto his back by my attack and I can hear his laugh in his chest where I've pressed my head against him. I turn to smell him, inhaling him like a dog.

'What was that for?' he demands, pulling me closer to him.

'I haven't seen you for a week,' I reply. 'And today is Tanabata. We're officially allowed to meet.' I continue my explorations, trying to stick my nose in his armpit as he bats me off, smelling his neck. 'Mizuki, that's disgusting.'

'No, it's good.' I can feel him against my hip, slide my hand down his front. 'You like it.'

'I like your everything,' he says, pulling my hand away. 'Stop.' He rolls on top of me, holding both my hands pinioned above my head. The taste of him fades the rest of the world into nothing.

'Why stop?' I demand, wriggling.

'Because some white-gloved dude with a peaked hat is going to come over and blow a whistle at us.'

'It's Yoyogi, not Shinjuku-Gyoen. There are perverts round here taking dodgy cosplay pictures all the time.'

'Yeah, that's different. Cosplay perverts are allowed.'

I turn my head to brush a piece of grass from my cheek and catch sight of something terrible on the path.

'Oh my god. Lie on top of me.'

'What?'

'Quick, quick, just lie on top of me so nobody can see me.'

Kiyoshi obliges.

'Don't move. Where are they going?'

'Who?'

'The women with the buggies. The one with the long skirt.' Ayaka, and Ichiko. The real Ichiko. I truly wonder, for the first time, what would happen if she knew I was saving Kiyoshi's number in my phone under her name, and the thought makes me smirk like a bad teenager.

Kiyoshi looks.

'They're walking down the path. They've stopped.'

'Oh god.'

I shift myself out from under Kiyoshi's weight slightly.

'Move so they can't see me.'

'Okay.' Kiyoshi rolls off and I inch towards the crook of his arm, where I can peer out without making myself visible.

We listen to each other breathing for a bit, and then Kiyoshi whispers, 'Who are they?'

I sigh. 'Mums of friends of Aki's. They're very nice.'

'But they would be surprised to see you rolling around on the grass with a man who isn't your husband?'

'Actually, they wouldn't know you're not my husband. Tatsu's never met any of them.' It's almost the only time his name has ever come up between us. 'They would probably be just as shocked if I was rolling around with my husband.'

'I see.'

'They're shocked by everything.' We're still whispering. 'Most things I say make them do that rabbit-in-the-headlights-sharp-intake-of-breath thing.'

'What do you say to the poor people?'

'Oh, you know. Very shocking things. That sometimes I'm over making bento and I wish Aki had school lunches already. Once, that I couldn't find a bikini I liked and did they know any nice swimsuit shops. I thought they were going to die.'

'A bikini?' Kiyoshi whispers in my ear. 'At your age? You slut.'

'That's what they think.' The women are settling themselves on the grass not ten metres away from us. 'Do any of your friends know?'

'About this?'

'Yes.'

'Only one. And Sotaro – I think he guessed.'

'Do they hate you?'

Kiyoshi gives me a strange look. 'Why would they hate me?' He puts a hand on my waist, shifting me closer to him. 'Doesn't make any difference to them.' He runs his hand along my stomach. 'They won't know you from the back. I'll stand behind you. Let's go. Come to mine.'

I don't need asking twice.

32

I guess he knew the rules, too. It would get to an afternoon, say, where it looked like we might be about to enter the territory of the doomed and the swooning. It's a feat not to, frankly, because the only people who ever have sex in the afternoons are inebriated or on drugs or having sex they're not meant to be having. Legitimate sex nearly always takes place in the evening. So I'd be pulling on my tights, thinking we might need to finish it just so we wouldn't have to be depressingly getting dressed at half past two in the afternoon, and Kiyoshi, like he smelt my mood, would suddenly be fully dressed and telling me some crackpot story, or hurrying me along because he had an insatiable need for a melon soda from a specific shop in Asakusa, and my melancholy would be blasted off the ground and I'd forget to end it.

In New York, I heard a lot about people who believed they deserved to be happy, often in tracksuits on chat shows. It's not that I think they don't, or that I don't. Or maybe not in the same way – I'm not an American, reciting self-love mantras at myself and with a debt of surprise parties and happy Christmases owed to me. Who 'deserves' to be happy? I live in Tokyo, not some poverty-stricken, war-torn nation; I have a family, a home, food, functioning society. I have so much. Reaching for anything else surely just makes me greedy.

It's not as if I have a burning desire to spend my allotted time on earth flagellating myself. Being happy would be preferable to not, for a million good reasons, the foremost of which has to be that happy people are nicer and more pleasant to be around. Less likely to give their offspring lasting psychological problems. But my deciding to be with Kiyoshi wouldn't make anyone happy. Not really. Not leaving the children, or bringing them with me and breaking their life; not the look on Tatsu's face that I'd never be able to forget; not wondering always, always, if I made the right decision or if I didn't and I'm selfish and I fucked everything up. Like so many other things, I can see how that would work for somebody else, but not for me.

How many times have I wished I could be outside myself, outside all my limitations and neuroses, so I could make a different decision and live a different life? Now, when I remember what I wanted before I met Kiyoshi, I think it was just to start over, to do it all again for the first time, or maybe not do it at all. To have a clean slate. To be somebody else. But then there would be no Aki, no Eri, and life doesn't work like that, does it? So I'm not leaving Tatsu for Kiyoshi, because that might be love, maybe, but it isn't happiness, not for me or for anybody else.

33

I haven't had a huge amount of sleep the morning Eri can't find her backpack. The thoughts keeping me awake were very much to do with her welfare, but not, it has to be said, as maternal or altruistic as might have been ideal. The moment I finally fell asleep, Aki came in. It is very difficult to sleep with a four-year-old determinedly plastered to your head, resisting all efforts to gently un-prise him, even in deepest sleep. I don't do very well on no sleep. It's one of many reasons that 'mother' might have been an unwise life choice. Aki has his shoes on and, bored of waiting for Eri, is throwing his hat up at the ceiling, then running to the other end of the genkan to catch it.

'Aki, can you stop that please.'

'But I like it.'

'That's irrelevant, unfortunately – you're going to break something. Stop.'

I call down the corridor. 'Eri, what are you doing? We're going to be late!'

Aki throws the hat so it lands on my face.

'Akihidé!' I peel the hat off and glare at him. I rarely

use his full name, and he looks interested. 'Eri! We need to leave!'

I can hear Eri stomping around like an angry cartoon. 'Where is it?' she thunders. 'Why can't I find it?'

'Find what?'

She comes storming out of her room and stands accusingly in front of me, her arms crossed and her eyes narrowed. She must stop watching manga. 'Where. Is. My. Bag?' she asks, in a threatening manner that would be comic if it weren't so infuriating.

'Eri, do not speak to me like that. I have no idea where your bag is. I am your mother, not your slave.' I can hear my voice rising. 'Stop standing there posing and find an alternative.' In my irritation, I grab her arm to pull it out of its crossed position. 'Go! Use your randoseru! We are leaving, and you have thirty seconds to meet us at the lift.'

I open the door and propel Aki in front of me. 'Come on, Aki.'

I turn to close the door and catch sight of Eri's face. Her arm is still hanging in a half-folded position. Her bottom lip is trembling and her mouth is twitching downwards at the edges.

'Eri, what's wrong?' She looks at me, and the action sends tears running down her cheeks.

'What is it?' My anger has dissipated instantly. I step forward to fold her into my arms. 'Eri-chan, what is it? It's all right.'

She resists for one moment, her body stiff, then leans into me, taking a ragged breath. I kiss the top of her head and sit down, cradling her in my lap like the baby she is, even with her gangly legs and school uniform. We sit for a moment, and Aki crawls round to stroke the top of Eri's head.

'What's wrong, Eri-chan? You don't have to tell me if you don't want to.'

She takes another breath. 'If I take my randoseru to school,' the thought of it sends a fresh wave of tears running down her cheeks, 'Sayuri will call me a baby.'

Damn Sayuri.

'Well, that sounds like a silly thing for Sayuri to say,' I tell her softly, rocking her.

'Sayuri always,' she heaves back a sob, 'she always tells the others I'm a baby. They laugh at me, Mama.'

I hold her tighter. 'They're a bunch of hyenas, Eri. What silly hyenas.'

'What's hyenas, Mama?' Aki wants to know.

'Silly animals who run around in packs, laughing at nothing.'

I am going to murder every last one of them.

I tell her that morning that school is hard for everyone, that school sometimes being a bit awful is basically an inevitable part of growing up. I tell her, not with as much vehemence or in language as powerful as I would like, that Sayuri is a lowly life form who isn't worth another glance, and that her best course of action is to ignore her completely and find someone different to hang out with. I tell her how much better it is to be laughed at by a bunch of morons than to somehow find yourself in a gang with a bunch of morons, laughing at nothing.

We find her old gym backpack and dig out a couple of souvenir key rings to hang off the zipper, and I promise to call the swimming pool to see if she left her backpack there. We're a few minutes late arriving at school and we have to go to the office to get a late slip, but no one died, and I'm not sure why it ever mattered so much that we might be late before. Eri smiles when I tell her I'll be there to pick her up, even though she's been coming home on the subway by herself for months now. After I've dropped off Aki and waved at him through the window, I call the only person in the world I want to speak to at that moment. Tatsuya.

That night he doesn't get back until late, and I'm in bed, trying to read. I can hear him going into Aki's room, tucking him up, and then I hear him go into Eri's room. He's in there for a while, silent, before he comes in and sits on the bed.

'I'm going to kill them.'

It's so in tune with my own thoughts that it makes me smile.

'How shall we do it?' I ask.

'I'm going to go into school with her tomorrow and throw them out of the window one by one.'

I laugh out loud.

'What?'

'Nothing. Just – usually it's me with the violent ideas and you're Mr Reasonable.'

'I am Mr Reasonable. That's a reasonable solution.'

We're silent for a moment.

'I think it's just a standard thing, isn't it?'

He nods, staring at his socked feet on the carpet. 'I got locked in the gym closet once, at school.' He throws himself backwards on the bed, rubbing his eyes. 'Oh god, that was a bad day.'

'Let's take them both out of school and move to Hawaii.

I'll teach them to hula dance on the beach, and you can fish. They don't need an education anyway.'

'We should never have had them, Mizu.'

'Why not?' I don't know why the question comes out sounding so sharp.

'They're too squidgy, and the world is too harsh.' He sits up. 'Squidgy Eri, and squidgy Aki.' He pats my leg through the covers. 'If we'd never had them, nobody could ever hurt them.' He sighs. 'I'm going to get in the bath.'

As he gets up, the lamplight catches the contours of his face. Poor Tatsu, he looks exhausted.

34

When I was pregnant with Eri and feeling pretty chipper about the situation, a mother with three children sighed and told me as if I would understand, 'The whole thing is heartbreaking.' No. Why would it be heartbreaking? New life, joy, the funny things toddlers do, surely the very opposite of heartbreaking? Surprisingly, I'm not indiscriminately into children and babies – kids, surely, are like people. Some of them are fantastic, and some of them are shitbags. I was expecting to be surrounded by mess, shouting, hopefully some amusement, but life, definitely, and a noisy one, which does not sound like heartbreak to me at all.

But as soon as the children were born it was blindingly obvious – your heart can't break unless it has something to love. The way you love your children, they take your heart with you everywhere they go. Suddenly you realise just how cruel, just how loud and brash and harsh and illogically cruel the world is, and it turns out that other mother was right. When they laugh, when they cry, when they're ill, when they grow, every moment they adore you and every step they take away from you – the whole thing is completely heartbreaking.

35

All of us were our parents' babies, once. That isn't ideal – I don't feel particularly comfortable communing with the thought that I suckled at my mother's breast. The realisation that at some point in the future my children will probably feel the same about me makes me feel gung-ho and sad in equal measure. But everyone is somebody's baby. Those grumpy old politicians, the check-out girl with the tic in the Lawson's down the road, the real Ichiko who drives me mad. Every single one moved a parent's heart to beat a little faster, to ache a little at the thought of their growing up. I was my parents' baby, their only child, and even though I think that all I did was be myself, I wish that I could take some of it back, or at least tell my dad I'm sorry.

Ultimately, I suspect my going to America was a mistake, although generally I try to avoid thinking that way. Presumably, if I hadn't gone, I never would have got it in my head that I wanted to sing. Which meant I would never have moved to New York or Tokyo alone instead of going to university like my dad so desperately wanted me to. This line of thinking inevitably concludes with

– and then maybe my dad wouldn't be dead. Do I really believe he died because I veered off the straight and narrow? Depends on the time of day, whose company I'm in. On a sunny morning, I could probably tell you he worked too hard, heart attacks are common as hell in a country that subsists on a diet of salt and stress; it was just a fact of life. Tragic, but the way it is. At 3 a.m., though, it's a different story. I remember my dad's bewildered look in the few days I was packing up to go back to New York, catching him sitting alone at the kotatsu staring at the table, the small glass of beer my mother had brought him untouched. His shoulders slightly stooped, but still smiling at me when I came in. He had a sister who lived in a village nearby, childless, kind enough in an abrasive sort of way. Loved a bit of melodrama. At his funeral, I heard her tell some random relative, with a hand on her chest, when she thought my mother and I couldn't hear, that my father had 'died of a broken heart'. Bitch.

My mum followed the Japanese rule book with her progeny. The rule is, modesty to the point of self-flagellation, and since our offspring are an extension of ourselves, everything they do is subpar. The way she talked about me, you would have thought I was mentally deficient and couldn't put one foot in front of the other. My dad, though, he didn't give a damn about that bit of the rule book; I was adored and mollycoddled, and his expression always reminded me of a happy manga character – two arches for his eyes and a smile that spread from ear to ear. He thought that I could be something, though he never specified what. When I haven't been paying strict enough attention to keep it under control, I've found myself wondering what would have been his ideal. He believed

I could excel, but he never wanted me far away. Maybe a doctor, working in the town's general hospital, or one of the scientists studying the dunes. Something in the local government, or a lawyer. Something with a name that made sense. 'Failed lounge singer with no further education' was definitely not on his list.

I was fifteen when he heard about the exchange. I never knew how he heard about it, since he was always in the shop one way or another, and his customers, with modal ages of seven or eighty-five, weren't the kind of people to be in the know about foreign exchange programmes for teenagers. Maybe he wrote to likely-sounding institutions or paid a trip to the university to ask for information. Alta Vista was just about available, but we didn't have a computer, and he wouldn't have known how to use one if we did.

Anyway, I got home from juku late one evening, and he was sitting at the kotatsu like someone about to explode with anticipation. He had the forms right there, crisp and white, and explained that I'd need transcripts of some of my exam papers, and which teachers I'd need to ask. He was so excited he practically filled the application in for me. I didn't really think I'd get in – America was just a word, and meant something huge, and far away, like the sun. After we'd posted the forms, I forgot about it completely, until the letter arrived. I remember I wanted to take the letter to my room, but my dad was looking at it so expectantly I couldn't, and had to open it right there in front of him, dreading the disappointed look on his face with every gummy rip of the envelope flap. The letter started by explaining how many applicants they'd had, so I familiarised myself with the sinking feeling and the slight quiet, until it said halfway down that I was one of the ones they'd selected to go. My dad just couldn't smile hard enough. The next evening he invited his sister over, and the cousins from my mum's side, and Onō-kun from the shop, and came home with Kentucky Fried Chicken and beer, and we all sat round the kotatsu making merry. Even now I think it was probably one of the best nights of my life.

I know I was the kid in my parents' family, and maybe that gives me more licence than I might give myself to have had my own ideas and run off to execute them. I guess that's what Cassie and her ilk would say, and the self-acceptance sex-line lady. But I was still responsible, for sure, for breaking that family. And I only have to think of my dad at the kotatsu, and my aunt's melodramatic voice, to know there's no way I could ever do it again.

36

Tokyo is in its full summer inferno when we meet one morning by Gaienmae. I've never much liked that avenue of trees, for all that it looks so spectacular. It's something about the government building at the bottom of it, its squatness, surrounded by so much space in a city where living quarters are measured out in mat sizes, making it seem like an overfed toad. Lording it over the trees, watching people as they enjoy their walks. Kiyoshi is quiet, brooding, and after not saying much, he sits down on a bench to have a cigarette.

'Work?' I ask him sympathetically.

'Mm. The New York project.' He's silent.

'What's up with it?' I prod.

'Deadlines. Always deadlines.'

'When are you next going?'

He sighs. 'They want me to be there next year.'

There's a pause.

'The whole of next year?'

'Yes.'

Oh.

'That's great,' I tell him earnestly, stealing his cigarette for a drag. 'That'll be so exciting for you.'

He looks at me with an expression that's hard to read.

'I'm not going, Mizuki.' The smoke gives me a second to answer.

'What do you mean?'

'I'm not going. I'm sending one of the managers over. Sotaro would be good. He'll like it out there too – young single guy.' He grins lasciviously.

'No, he won't,' I say automatically. 'He's a Japanese single guy and he doesn't speak English very well. He'll just work his balls off and the Western women will scare him.'

Kiyoshi rolls his eyes at me. 'Fine, I'll send Hirota then. His wife will love it. She can go shopping on Fifth Avenue. Happy?'

'Why aren't you going? You were so excited about it.'

'I have shit to do here. The other restaurants need looking after.'

'No, they don't, they function perfectly. You just stick your nose in once in a while to remind them you're a control freak.'

He smiles, but it falls down. 'Yeah, well.'

'Kiyoshi.' I can't say it.

He sits up straighter. 'What?' It's aggressive.

'Don't—'

'Don't what?'

'Don't let me get in the way of your plans.'

He barks out a humourless laugh. 'Don't flatter yourself.'

'Nice.'

I turn away from him and look up at the leaves of the ginkgo tree above us. The cicadas are humming, the sound of summer, insistent.

'You're already in the way of my plans.' His voice is harsh, robotic.

'Well, I can get out of the way easily enough.' He doesn't say anything, so I stand up.

He moves his head in a weary action, like I'm another in a long line of women who have behaved in a certain way.

'Bye,' I say, aware I'm acting like a child. It seems laughable to be so petty when the sun is shining so brilliantly.

'Mizuki, for god's sake.'

'I don't want to get in the way.' I start walking quickly.

'Mizuki, wait.' He stands up and starts after me. 'I'm sorry.'

I stop. The words are hard to form. 'You know—' They won't come. 'I can't. This won't . . .'

'I know.' His face is angry. 'You know I know. I've always known.'

'So go to New York.' The words are overbright, the inside of my chest a chasm. 'It'll be amazing. You have to watch it get built. You have to go.'

'Don't tell me what I have to do!' He spits the words out. He looks away, then seems to think of something that makes him even angrier. He takes a step towards me, all his height and strength and energy against me. 'You. Do not. Get to tell me what to do.'

I blink back tears. 'I know that,' and my voice sounds very small. I start to walk away again, willing myself not to cry.

He's next to me a few moments later, grabbing my hand to make me stop. I try to shake him off, not wanting him to see my face. 'Let go,' and my voice is so full of tears it sounds ridiculous.

'I'm sorry, Mizuki, I'm so sorry,' and I press my face into him with his arms around me. I know it has started, the end of it, like we always knew it would. The end of it was in the beginning of it. I love you, I want to tell him, even though I never said it. I love you so much, and it isn't any use to anybody.

37

A lover's tiff that ends in great sex isn't the same as knowing each other through a decade of children shouting at you. I know that. It's not that I'm recommending the latter over the former; it's just that I'm not under the illusion that Kiyoshi and I had any smaller chance of falling into a bickering hole than anyone else did, if we'd had an ordinary domestic life. But I suppose that's part of love, or young love anyway – the deep desire to roll the dice and find out, always with the absurd hope, flying like a kite, that you might just be the ones who manage to hold onto each other through it all. Once, when I was thinking of something else, I had a fleeting image of a parallel universe where Kiyoshi and I had built our life, and the way he held our child. I quashed it.

38

'Mama, Aki kicked me.' Eri hisses with rage, old enough (and female enough) to be highly conditioned to appropriate subway behaviour, but furious nonetheless. She is sitting with her knees and feet together, her bag perched on her bright, yukata'd lap, her hair brushed and shining, half of it in a neat plait tied with a star-shaped bobble, her beloved jelly shoes, silver glitter set in translucent plastic, immaculate. She is every inch a perfectly blend-in-able Tokyoite. My daughter. With a streak of her mother's uncontrollable temper, poor thing. I find myself trying not to smile and she glares at me with a yet more towering indignation. She is going to be formidable.

'Aki, stop that,' I whisper, 'or we're going to have to swap places.' Aki is sitting between Eri and me, very pleased with his position, swinging his legs and humming to himself. At the mention of swapping, he goes instantly still and clutches Eri's forearm.

'No.'

It only takes ten seconds for him to start again, drumming his feet happily against his seat.

'Do you see anyone else kicking each other in this

carriage?' Aki looks around pointlessly. Two young girls also in yukata are giggling with each other, and a pair of elderly women in stretch trousers and hiking hats are discussing their descent of Mount Takao. The row of people in front of us are wearing face masks, all resting their eyes while sitting bolt upright. Although face masks are undeniably hygienic, I have a fleeting, Western-brained thought that the image is mildly horrific, apocalyptic.

'No.' He looks disappointed.

'They are all having a peaceful time, and you mustn't disturb them.'

Eri gives me a grown-up look. 'We are approaching Azabu-jūban,' she says, 'so we have five stops left.'

'Is it Azabu? I didn't hear the announcement.'

'There was no announcement,' she tells me witheringly. 'It's the tune for Azabu-jūban,' indicating with her head the barely perceptible jingle being piped through the train's tannoy. Aki hums along in agreement. It disturbs me to find that my children have been programmed by the Tokyo Metro system. We pull into the station and more girls in yukata trip onto the train, their gait made even more coy than usual by the wooden geta held to their feet with vermillion straps. They twitter happily to each other like the birds they resemble, flamboyant swathes of pattern and colour.

Aki pushes himself out of his chair to whisper in my ear. 'Mama, are those ladies,' he indicates with his eyes, 'going to the omatsuri too?'

'Maybe,' I whisper back. 'It's a very big omatsuri.'

'Can I have kakigōri when we get there? A strawberry one?' Nothing is better than the shaved ice in the summer heat.

'Of course.'

'Do they know I'm going to the omatsuri, because I'm in my jinbei?' He slides off his seat to stand, the better for me to admire his matching traditional kimono top and shorts, navy blue with a repeated pattern of tiny white rabbits and moons. I lament that this will be the last year they will fit him.

'They might do. It makes you look very handsome.'

'But I wanted to wear my yukata,' Aki says sadly.

'It's still too big, Aki. You can wear it next year.'

'It won't make me look like a girl?'

'How could you look like a girl? Men wear yukatas too.'

'Papa doesn't.'

Papa used to, I start to tell him, when he had time to change into one instead of always rushing everywhere straight from work, so he looks melded into his suit. But instead I say, 'That man is, over there,' indicating a smiling youth with dyed blond hair and a paper fan tucked into the back of his obi belt. 'Anyway, yours is a boy's one, with dragonflies.' The train starts to pull out of the station.

'And fireworks,' he looks at Eri's yukata, and then mine, 'and flowers are for girls. But I like fireworks and flowers. Don't you like dragonflies?'

'Really,' I tell him, pulling him onto my lap, 'I think everything is for everyone, girls and boys. Don't you?'

Obon is nearing, the festival of the dead, when they come back across the water (from where, exactly? Korea? Russia?) for three days to visit the living. I think of my mother at home, who will spend days arduously cooking all my father's favourite foods. Her korokke, crispy on the outside and soft as clouds inside, flame-cooked aubergines with ginger, their blackened skins peeled off like shells, bowls of plain white rice with her homemade pickles. Washing my father's grave, tutting to him about the heat and making sure the water is cool enough for him, placing fresh-cut irises in front and lighting the lamps that flank it. My father always loved the bon-odori in our town, the spectacular dance that makes its way through the streets, the colourful paper and bamboo umbrellas of the dancers spinning, their shouts and the sound of taiko-drumming filling the air.

Will he be watching? At Obon, it's as easy to believe that he will, that the mukaebi lanterns lit inside our home will guide him back as they're supposed to, as it is impossible to believe anything like it the rest of the year. Tonight, at the omatsuri, there will be striped red and white stalls lit with strings of electric lights, the cooks with their traditional headbands, sweating over griddles to flip savoury pancakes and scribble up woks of fried noodles, and coax spherical puffs of octopus and batter from their moulds. Beads of condensation will roll down the sides of cold glass bottles of ramune, the fizzy drink with the marble stopping up its mouth to jangle enticingly in the bottle as you drink, and all the workers manning their stalls will be calling out their wares with all their might, adding their voices to the sounds of lutes and shamisen, bells and excited chanting accompanying the mikoshi being carried aloft by muscular shoulders to the shrine.

'I love omatsuri, Mama,' Aki tells me confidingly.

'Me too,' I say, squeezing him.

'Can we stay for the fireworks?'

'Of course.' That's when the train comes to an apologetic halt.

The carriage is swaying in the wrong direction. The sleepers, who would keep their eyes shut through all the expected commotion of a station stop, come to and look around surreptitiously. The chatter of the young people dies down. For a moment, nobody speaks, complicit in the hope that the swaying is a result of the brakes and can somehow be explained away. There is a violent lurch, and the hand straps hanging from the ceiling swing ominously from side to side.

'Is it an earthquake, Mama?' Aki asks with interest. I reach over to take Eri's hand. Her eyes have become very big, and she grips my hand tightly.

'Maybe,' I say, surprised by the calmness of my tone. 'Nothing to worry about.'

The carriage continues to shudder, and nobody moves. This is what we always do, say nothing, accept our fate, the fact we have always known that this was on the cards. Underground, though, stoicism is harder. One of the women in the hiking hats calls over to someone at the other end.

'Can you open the door?' Her voice is friendly, as if she's asking for a favour.

The other half of the carriage is still in the station. A suited man standing by a door presses the open button to no avail. As the shuddering jostles another passenger against him, he tries again, and again.

'It won't open.' A sound, a cross between an exhalation and a sob, escapes from one of the young girls and she puts her hand over her mouth.

'Mama,' Eri says, and the word is drawn-out, her eyes on mine. She doesn't look grown-up any more. She looks like a terrified little girl.

'Don't worry, Eri-chan,' I say, pulling her close. 'Everything's fine.'

Aki turns and puts his arms around my neck, the carriage jerking us this way and that. The pressure of the children's bodies against mine makes me realise how shallow my breathing is. I can hear people shouting in the carriages further down the tunnel and see that the lights have gone out.

Belatedly, the safety systems on people's mobile phones spring into action, telling us that we are experiencing an earthquake. The driver's voice comes over the tannoy to tell us the same thing and entreat us to stay calm. He apologises for the inconvenience, as if seismic forces were something within his control which he had accidentally overlooked, and suggests we remain seated.

I can feel Eri and Aki's breathing warm against my cheek and ear and think of Kiyoshi's friend in the second tower. Like hell we're just going to sit here. I stand up, sliding Aki to his feet, unsteady on my own, gripping the children's hands.

'Everything's fine,' I reassure them again, talking to Eri as if she is Aki's age. 'We're just going to go over here and see what's going on.'

All the earthquake drills of our lives have told us to get underneath things, to stand in door frames, but here there is nothing to get under, nothing to stand in. I cross the hands holding each of theirs so that the three of us advance as one being, bending to shield them under me as much as I can. The lights at the end of our carriage flicker. We reach the doors that are still in the station and I pause, at a loss. In the station, the vending machine is juddering and the cavernous space makes me very aware of the height of the ceiling. People have folded themselves into the tiny spaces under seats, or are crouched or sitting, arms and bags protecting their heads. Where are we safest? What is less likely to fall, to break, to cave in? As I place my hand on the crack between the doors, the carriage gives an almighty lurch, and something crashes to the floor, right where the three of us were sitting moments before. In the second before the light goes out, I see that the cover has fallen off and is swaying like a half-amputated limb, thumping against the seat where Eri had been sitting. The children are shocked into silence, staring at me, their eyes enormous. The swaying slows and comes to a stop. In the quiet that follows, we hear the threatening creaks of unknown things, and the suppressed sobbing of the girl.

I press the button for the doors again. Nothing. The driver is back on the speaker, but all I can see in my mind is Aki and Eri in the open with nothing to fall on them. I force my fingers into the minuscule gap between the doors and pull with all my might, my fingers feeling that they might dislocate. The door gives a couple of centimetres. Without a word, the man standing opposite me starts to pull at the other door, and someone else materialises to help me pull on my side. My shoulders burn, my arms are numb. Every gram of my being is focused on opening the doors, all the fury and strength that has ever been in me. If they don't open, we will smash the windows. We are leaving this station before anything else happens; before the station realises what hit it and crumbles in on itself, or an aftershock arrives. We are getting out. Painful centimetre by centimetre, the door grinds open. As soon as it's wide enough, I grab both children's hands in one of mine.

'Come on, Aki,' I croon, squeezing sideways out of the gap. 'Eri, off we go.' As if I am strapping them into their buggies and not feeling as if the bottom is about to fall out of my stomach. 'We're going to go very quickly now, okay? Nothing to worry about, we're just in a bit of a hurry.'

I take a firm grip of Eri's hand and pick Aki up; he wraps his legs around my waist like a monkey. Others have squeezed out of the gap and rush silently past us. As we hurry along, I curse the fact I am wearing my yukata, the shape of it restricting my movements. Towards the exit, up the tiled stairs, not thinking, just getting out. Everything will be fine. Keep going, up the stairs, down a corridor, wondering if that's another tremor or just my imagination. Doesn't matter, keep going. How far underground is Azabu-jūban? Don't worry, don't think, just go.

'It's all right,' I'm muttering to Aki. 'Everything's fine.'

'Mama,' Eri is panting. 'You're going too fast, there are too many stairs.'

'I know, Eri-chan, but we can't stop, only a few more now.' I can feel her slowing minutely. 'I mean it, Eri, we're not stopping.'

I'm practically pulling her arm out of its socket with the force of dragging her along. The straps of my geta are digging in and I realise I would be quicker without them, but I can't waste the few seconds it would take to kick them off. The thought makes me trip along faster, the throbbing in my feet spurring on yet another flood of adrenaline. Up the stationary escalators, dull pain running through my legs. The tremor can no longer be ignored; the steps are jiggling under us and in the moment that I take in the light fittings on the ceilings, the tiles on the walls, I wonder if I have made a terrible mistake.

'Mama, stop,' Eri begs. 'It hurts, stop.'

'We can't stop, Eri,' I tell her. 'Come on, you're doing so well.'

Aki has started to slide off my waist and I shift him so I am holding him under one arm, balancing him on my hip like a piece of luggage. He doesn't complain. I'm aware we're going more slowly than the people who have materialised behind us, and redouble my efforts. My back is drenched in sweat and the escalator extends endlessly above us. Please let the exit be at the top of this one. Please, please. By the time we reach the top Aki is practically on the floor, and I nearly drop him onto the ground. He springs up and grabs my hand.

Exit signs are pointing in all directions, like a Wonderland nightmare. The tannoy has switched to an automated voice and is informing us on repeat that we are experiencing an earthquake. In the moment I spend dithering about which exit to take, I look down at the children, huddled against my legs. They are both looking up at me expectantly, and even in the midst of it all, Aki smiles at me.

'Exit One,' I decide. 'It has to be Exit One.' I pick Aki up and we set off.

'Mama, it's not fair,' Eri whimpers, sounding close to tears. 'Why can't you pick me up?'

'I wish I could,' I tell her, and I have never wished anything more fervently than that I could scoop them both up in my arms and sprint. 'Only a little further now, nearly there.'

The tremors have become more violent. In any other earthquake, not trapped underground, we would never clamber up those undulating stairs, straight past the lady with the bleeding head and the man she is leaning on, except that now I have seen daylight. When we finally reach the top, my legs can't compute the flat ground and I nearly fall to the floor. The metallic taste in my mouth is so strong I find myself dry heaving as we throw ourselves through the open ticket barriers. Station guards are standing at their posts looking shell-shocked as clusters of people surge through; there must be people still trapped in the train, miles below us.

On the street, cars are stationary in the road, and water is leaking out of cracks that have appeared in the ground, as if the earth is weeping. I totter to a car in the middle of the road, as far away from buildings as we can be in Tokyo, and sink down next to it, pulling the children with me. Eri is panting, but Aki is still refreshed enough to be interested. 'Why are we sitting down in the middle of the road, Mama? Have all the cars stopped because of the earthquake?'

'My chest hurts,' Eri says, burying her head in my side. 'And my legs.'

I suddenly discover that I don't have enough breath to speak, and that my insides are so churned up I might vomit. 'You were so brave,' I manage to choke out. 'You both did such a good job.'

Finally, the tremors slow and the world is eerily quiet. I notice that other people are crouching by the cars too. 'Look at the sky,' I say to the children, for no reason other than that we are no longer underground, and that endless blue has never looked so inviting.

We sit in silence for what seems an eternity, the whole world poised for another onslaught, a pause in some surreal cosmic battle. The strange limbo is broken by the sound of a phone ringing, first one, then another and another as the network rights itself. One is particularly insistent, but it's only when Eri points it out that I realise it's mine. It's Tatsu.

'Are you okay? Are the kids okay?'

'Yes,' and the tears come like a dam breaking. 'We're fine.'

When eventually I have recovered my senses enough to realise that Eri and Aki have both folded into me, Eri with both her arms around mine and Aki with his face buried in my lap, I laugh through my snot and tears and hold them close.

'Were you scared, Mama?' Aki asks.

'Yes,' and I kiss the perfection of his round cheek. 'I was very scared.'

39

My phone rings at 2 a.m. that night, which it never has before, showing Ichiko on the caller ID. It's on silent but I'm awake, curled up next to Tatsu, listening to him breathing. It's been years since I slept so close to him, but tonight I've been in and out of bed, going to check on Eri, going to check on Aki, and since I can't sleep next to them both simultaneously, something draws me to put my arm around Tatsu. Their Papa. Across the city, there have been many casualties but only a handful of deaths reported so far. Tonight, people whose homes have become unsafe, or who lack electricity and water, are bedding down in the gymnasiums of local schools, news reports showing grannies smiling in their neatly arranged beds. There's footage of a park in the outskirts of the city, where the buildings were old and haven't fared well, where the underground toilets have materialised as planned, and the children on camera who have been evacuated appear as excited as if they're on a school camping trip.

I want to tell Kiyoshi about it, ask him if he's seen it, and keep pushing away the thought of him under rubble, alone. I've tried to check the neighbourhoods where Gion and Kami are situated on the earthquake maps that tally the destruction, but not everything is updating. Ginza, where Gion is situated, is an old neighbourhood full of tall buildings, the worst kind of place to be. It's unlikely, I tell myself, and with the ground solid beneath our feet, even if only temporarily, it's easy to scold myself for being overdramatic. Yet as I hold the children too close to me, so that they squirm to get away, I'm distracted by a vertiginous feeling, a panic that I don't want to acknowledge.

Tatsu was in the office when the earthquake hit. He told me after the children had gone to bed about filing cabinets flying across the room and not being able to tear himself away from his window, watching the city undulating with Namazu's thrashings beneath it.

'Were you scared?' I ask him, just as the children asked me.

'Kind of. I figured it was binary. Either we were all going to be fine or the building was going to collapse and that would be the end of it.' It's mysterious to me how this conclusion would lead only to ambivalent fear.

'I was more scared something would happen to the kids,' he says. 'To you.'

In sleep, he pats my arm, holds my hand, shifts so that we spoon closer, like we did at the beginning. As if the rift of the last half decade never happened, or he didn't notice it. When the blue light of my phone illuminates the ceiling, Tatsu doesn't stir. I run as silently as I can into the sitting room.

'Yes?' I whisper into the receiver. I haven't heard from him since the earthquake, haven't been able to get through to him. Staring at the number saved under Ichiko's name on my phone this evening, in the midst of everything else,

I've come to wonder if Kiyoshi is a figment of my imagination. If the string of numbers I don't even know off by heart is a hoax or a fantasy, and my messages and phone calls are disappearing into the ether. Even as I pick up, I'm not quite sure who will be at the other end.

'You're okay,' Kiyoshi says, and in the pause I know that he has run his fingers over his eyes, and through his hair. 'I couldn't get through to you.' The sound of his voice.

'Yes.' Apparently, there haven't been enough tears already. 'And you are. I thought you were dead. I thought I made you up.'

'You didn't make me up, Mizuki,' and he's laughing a little. 'I'm here. Where were you? Are you okay?'

'I was with the children, in the Metro.'

'Are they okay?' The question is instantaneous, alert, for two people he has never met.

'They're fine. We were in the station; we ran up the stairs. They did really well.' I have to stop. 'Are you okay? Where were you?'

'Visiting my mum.'

'I'm glad you weren't in Gion. It's so high.'

'Yeah. Probably the best place you could be, in a cemetery.' There's a pause, then Kiyoshi starts to laugh again. 'But then when I was going back to town, I remembered my summer jobs in construction when I was a teenager, and how I slapped buildings together without a clue what I was doing. I thought the whole place might be squashed flat when I got back. The ultimate comeuppance.'

I smile for the first time since the earthquake. 'Fuck. It really would be. Where are you now?'

'At my brother's.' He tuts in annoyance. 'They're

probably going to have to take down my apartment in Tokyo, now. They've been threatening to do it for months.'

I wish everything could go back to before the earthquake. I wish I could carry on listening to his voice, and laughing, and feeling better.

'Are you okay?' He says again, and he's not asking about the earthquake, not really.

'Yes.' The image that has been keeping me awake is of the children's faces in the moment I tried to decide which exit to take. Aki smiling at me even as everything was shaking around us, both with absolute faith in my ability to keep them safe. I've been existing in two realities, and my children can only be in one of them.

'I missed you,' I tell him, but the words are inadequate. I thought he was lost already.

'Me too,' he says, and I think he knows.

After we hang up, I sit for a long time staring at the city glittering below me, the cars pulsing past on the motorway. Like the lifeblood of the city, they don't slow, or decrease, just because it's 3 a.m. and Tokyo nearly collapsed today. Nearly, but it didn't, and now the show must go on.

They don't have earthquakes, do they, in New York? I never felt one in the years I was there. I'm glad. I send Kiyoshi a message asking if we can meet tomorrow at the cemetery in Nezu, somewhere far away, where I won't need to go for a while. Then, like the responsible citizen I am, I push my phone off the balcony.

40

When Laurence tells me he is moving to Osaka, I am relieved.

'I wanted to thank you, Mizuki, for all your help. It's been truly invaluable.'

Truly invaluable. I love English.

I tell him, in all sincerity, that it's been a pleasure, that I'll be sad not to see him any more. I'll get set up with another hapless foreigner, a newborn chick taking its first tentative steps and blinking in the land of the rising sun. Maybe it will give me something to focus on, meeting someone new and opening this parallel universe up to them. Or maybe I'm done with this job and I'll start doing something else. Go the other way, teach English to indoc- trinated housewives who want to break free. Who knows.

'What will you be doing in Osaka?'

'My company has an office there, so similar to what I do here,' Laurence says. After all this time, I'd be hard-pressed to specify exactly what that is. 'My girlfriend,' a shy smile plays at the corner of his lips as he says it, 'she's from Osaka originally and she wants to go back.'

'She's Japanese?'

'Yes. I could never have got together with her if you hadn't taught me so well.' It sounds like I've been giving him pick-up techniques, and I laugh. I start to imagine what it would be like to have a foreign boyfriend, then a foreign husband, but the line of thought is painful, somehow.

We talk a little more and, when our hour is up, I bow to him but Laurence folds me into a hug. I'm taken aback, but the freshly laundered smell of him, his long arms around me, are immediately comforting. Another person, with another life. I have cash this time and insist on paying for him, to make up for the time he paid. That time. As I go to push open the door, I glance behind me once. I'll change the venue for my next set of lessons, I think.

41

I was early arriving at Nezu, early for the first time since we'd met, and when he found me, he sat down next to me. There was a breeze ruffling the leaves of the trees, and the cicadas were singing. Children swept past on their bicycles, people wandered the paths among the graves, enjoying the shade. The grave in front of us was wet where someone had poured water over it to cool it down in the summer heat.

'I can't.'

He looked at me for a long time.

'I understand,' he said, and kissed my forehead, his hand on the nape of my neck.

'I'm sorry,' I tried to say, but it wouldn't come out. He made a noise that was half a sigh, half a laugh.

'I'll never be sorry,' he told me, and then he stood up and walked away.

I closed my eyes and tried to think of my children's faces to stop myself running after him. When I opened them, he had gone.

42

There it is. There's that over, and I'm here, and he's – wherever he is. I passed his building once, accidentally, and it wasn't there any more. Like the tree falling in the wood with no one to hear it, it's as if nothing ever happened. Perhaps I did make him up. Or else he's somewhere, still existing, still under the same sun, and the same moon, and happy, hopefully. And up I get, dust myself off, open the metaphorical curtains and get on with being happy too. I look around and there they still are – my beautiful children, my beautiful husband, my beautiful life. Did anyone ever deserve them less?

Eloise is teaching me French now, because why the hell not? In an ideal world, of course, it wouldn't be French, but it's not as if someone can own an entire language, an entire country. We meet on Saturday mornings, taking turns to find brunch places, while Tatsu takes the kids to the park, or swimming. I thought it was going to be a harder sell than it was, but Tatsu was easy; he's never not wanted to spend time with the kids. Eri and Aki wake up even earlier than usual on a Saturday now, brimming with overexcitement at spending the morning with Papa.

Brunch is definitely my favourite meal of the day; its optimism and energy, the wholesome anticipation of the sunny day ahead. It feels like a cheerful resolution, weekly fuel for a new beginning. My French accent isn't much better than when I made my poor attempts at it in New York, and my frustration makes Eloise laugh. I think there was a time when I would have minded her laughing, but I'm trying to wear myself more lightly these days, and I laugh too. On the days I wake up to find a weight I don't want to think about pressing down on me, I think of Eloise teasing me, and I can get up and smile.

There's such a lot to smile about. We have a new family member, Pocari the hamster, a birthday present for Aki that I slightly fear he's going to love to death. I've capitulated to Eri's fantasies and promised I'll take her to Paris, though it'll have to be when I can get some time off. Just after Laurence left, a position opened up for an interpreter, which was kind of what I'd been doing all the time anyway. The difference is that now two days a week I leave the house in heels and Elena collects Aki from school. Part-time jobs are gold dust, and I tell Eloise she's my fairy godmother, which she assures me is ridiculous. Proving that despite all my tuition and her years of living here, she still doesn't really understand what it's all about. Tatsu's mother has become increasingly thin-lipped towards me since I took the job, but her son is perfectly equable with the arrangement.

'The children seem happy,' was all he said when I asked him about it once. 'And you seem happy too. So I'm happy.' This conversation took place on the terrace one evening, when my husband was not checking his emails or looking at his phone, but at me, and at the view. Sometimes when he looks at me, I wonder if he can see where I've been, if he knows what I've felt. It makes me wonder what I don't know about him, too, and the thought makes me feel, oddly, closer to him; it reminds me of us at the beginning, when we chose what to reveal and had the courtesy of shielding each other from things that were unpalatable, of being our best selves for the other, instead of knowing too much. We're not sailing into the sunset; Tatsu still works insane hours and will probably carry on that way until he retires to play golf. I haven't had a lobotomy that has suddenly turned me into a winsome doormat. I look at his profile, his eyelashes against his cheekbones, the hair at his temples that is starting to be flecked with strands of grey and remember when I first met him, when everything was jet-black. I never imagined then that I would know him so long, or so well. We're adults, and we've built something, and we've both felt how precarious this life can be.

Eri and I discuss Paris like it's our honeymoon. We're going to go up the Eiffel Tower twice, once during the day and once at night, and we're going to stay in Montmartre and eat croissants and go to restaurants where the menu is written up on blackboards, and Eri is going to buy a school bag that will make Sayuri expire of envy on the spot. It's going to be so fantastic Tatsu and Aki are threatening to come too.

Sometimes, the taste of something or a building in the distance catches me unawares; Tokyo is full of traps. There's an ema from a shrine with a snow monkey on it that sits on a bookshelf in the sitting room; there are no wishes or prayers written on the back, and I put it in plain sight because I wanted to believe there was nothing to hide. It's a beautiful object, and it's starting to blend into the background. I'm waiting for the day when I won't see it any more, or, when I do, it will only be to admire the craftsmanship of the painting, the delicate wood. I saw the old lady in the supermarket again one day, when Aki and I stopped in to get some bean sprouts after I'd collected him from school. I helped her reach a packet of katsuobushi from a high shelf, and she told Aki how grand he looked in his uniform. I wonder what will still matter when I'm as old as she is. I wonder who she loved, and what she hid, and when it stopped hurting her to remember, even while she was pretending to have forgotten.

My family will still matter; my children. They're all I'm thinking about now; the thud of Aki's wriggly little body as he throws himself into my arms for a hug, about how seeing Eri laugh with her nose wrinkled up makes me love her so much it hurts my chest. About Shinjuku-Gyoen picnics and the beach, and Tatsu's face on the pillow in the morning. And the blameless loveliness of watching Ghibli films on a Saturday night and jelly shoes at the front door. And all the love there is in my life.

And you, and you, and you.

ACKNOWLEDGEMENTS

Thank you so much to my wonderful agent Kirsty McLachlan for believing in what was originally 'Ballad'; I still have to pinch myself frequently. To Francesca Main for her wisdom, warmth and skill; working with her on this book has been the greatest pleasure and privilege. To Steve Marking and Holly Ovenden for the beautiful cover, Cait Davies, Kate Moreton, Loz Jerram, Rosie Pearce, Jessica Purdue, Virginia Woolstencroft and all of the incredible team at Phoenix and Orion who have made the book world such an exciting place to come into, even at a time when it sometimes felt like the real world was falling apart. To Katherine Nintzel and the team at Custom House, particularly Mumtaz Mustafa for a cover that makes me even more desperate to go out in Tokyo again; Eliza Rosenberry and Danielle Finnegan, I'm so happy about the book hopping over the pond and being in such good hands. To Irene for reading things even when they have way too much swearing in them and picking me up over decades. To the unique and fabulous parentals for not appearing to mind what random choices I made, and letting me gerronwithit. To the Wus for the title ideas, the noise and the glamour; without you, things would take a quarter of the time to finish, and have no point at all. To Tim, for the possibilities, the laughs, for everything. And to Naomi, for always getting all of it.